ROXANN DELANEY

doesn't remember a time when she wasn't reading or writing, and she always loved that touch of romance in both. A native Kansan, she's lived on a farm, in a small town and has returned to live in the city where she was born. Her four daughters and grandchildren keep her busy when she isn't writing or designing websites. The 1999 Maggie Award winner is excited to be a part of the Mills & Boon® Cherish line and loves to hear from readers. Contact her at roxann@roxanndelaney.com or visit her website, www.roxanndelaney.com

For all those who are a part of the
adoption triad—adoptees, adoptive
parents and birth parents—
may your lives be filled with love,
understanding and acceptance.

The Cowboy Meets His Match

ROXANN DELANEY

First published in Great Britain 2014
by Mills & Boon, an imprint of Harlequin (UK) Limited,
Large Print edition 2014
Eton House, 18-24 Paradise Road,
Richmond, Surrey, TW9 1SR

ISBN: 978-0-263-23936-2

Harlequin (UK) Limited's policy is to use papers that are natural, renewable and recyclable products and made from wood grown in sustainable forests. The logging and manufacturing processes conform to the legal environmental regulations of the country of origin.

Printed and bound in Great Britain
by CPI Antony Rowe, Chippenham, Wiltshire

Chapter One

Stretching out her legs in the tall grass, with her eyes closed and her back against the rough bark of a tree, Erin Walker smiled at the sound of a fish breaking the surface of the water. Content, she pulled in a breath of warm, June afternoon air and started to toe off her boots. But the sound of a second, a third and then a fourth splash followed, all louder and each sounding closer than the one before.

That was no fish.

She sat up straight, her heart rate increasing as she looked out onto Lake Walker, the large pond on the ranch near Desperation, Oklahoma, where she'd grown up. That was when she spotted the naked man, standing not twenty yards away in the pond.

Erin felt an eerie flash of déjà vu but blamed it on the shock of the moment. Surely he hadn't seen her. If he had, he would have left immediately. Instead, he stood hip deep in the water, his back to her, his arms stretched above his head, flexing muscles that would have caused a half-blind ninety-year-old spinster to suffer a case of the vapors.

If only he'd turn around.

Just as she finished the thought, he started to do exactly that. She quickly but carefully scooted down to lie on the ground, while praying he was too busy enjoying his skinny-dip to notice her. From her prone position, all she could see was the very top of his head—and that was only if she stretched her neck uncomfortably. She was also aware that if she moved, he might notice her. With a silent sigh, she lowered her head, settling in to wait him out.

Closing her eyes so she could concentrate on

any sounds, she yawned, her previous late night catching up with her early morning. After a few minutes, she heard the sound of movement in the water. He was leaving. Or maybe coming closer. She couldn't be certain, but the sound seemed to be getting farther and farther away, until it stopped. Straining to listen for confirmation, she thought she heard the soft whinny of a horse, but she couldn't be certain.

More time passed, as she waited for some kind of indication that he was no longer in the area. When she heard nothing else, she finally felt relatively safe.

"Did you enjoy the view?"

She froze. She knew that voice, would never forget it and was trapped by the person it belonged to. She suspected he was waiting for an answer, but she needed time to settle the slamming of her heart and attend to her need to breathe. The first was impossible; the second was achieved by forcing air into her lungs.

She refused to open her eyes, her heart pounding in her ears as she struggled to gain control. When she finally opened them, there was no one there. No person, no horse, no evidence that what she'd heard had been real. For all she knew, she'd fallen asleep and dreamed it. If so, it had been her worst nightmare.

In spite of being fairly certain she'd imagined the whole thing, she remained cautious as she got to her feet. The first thing she did was check to make sure no one was lurking behind her in the bushes, but there was nobody there.

"No, it didn't happen," she muttered.

She used the walk back to her childhood home—now her brother's house—to clear her head. She'd been dreaming. That had to be it. But why? It had been years since—

Unwilling to think about what had happened long ago, she forced her thoughts to something else. When she first decided to visit Lake Walker, she'd thought she would do some riding, but the idea of saddling and mounting the horse that had replaced Firewind only made her miss him that much more. Erin prided herself on not being particularly emotional, and she didn't want to give herself any reason to get that way, so she'd chosen to walk instead. She welcomed the exercise. She hadn't been sleeping well for weeks, and she'd been so tired lately—it made sense that she'd imagined someone had spoken to her, although the man in the pond had definitely been real.

Back at the house, she stepped inside the screened porch, then opened the door that led into the kitchen, where she found both of her brothers seated at the table. "I see you took—"

"It's about time you got back here," Luke, the youngest, announced.

She looked first at him and then at Dylan, who scowled at her. "What?" she asked. "I'm not allowed to get some exercise?"

Dylan leaned back in his chair, his scowl deepening. "We have somewhere to go. *We* meaning you, too."

"Did you forget?" Luke asked.

She *had* forgotten, but they didn't need to know that, now that they'd reminded her. "Of course not. We're meeting up with the others at Lou's Place."

"Right." Dylan crossed his arms on his chest. "And we're expected to be there in thirty minutes."

"No problem," she replied. "It won't take me long to get cleaned up and—"

"Dean is expecting to meet you there."

She stared at Luke, hoping her confusion appeared believable. "Dean? Dean who?"

"You know damn well who," Dylan said. Pushing away from the table, he stood and walked over to her, his six-foot-plus body towering over her. "Dean Franklin. You remember him. We introduced you to him at the fall festival last October."

"I have no idea who you're talking about." No way would she let herself be set up with another man her brothers had chosen for her. And if they insisted, she would pack up her motor home and leave. She had plenty of friends on the rodeo circuit who would be happy to give her a place to park until she found somewhere permanent to live. For that to happen, she needed money, and she refused to ask her brothers for it.

"You agreed to meet him," Luke said.

Erin shook her head. "No. You—both of you—set it up and told him I'd be there. I never had a say in it or in the other men you've tried to marry me off to since the leaves started falling from the trees last October. Give it up, boys. I've had enough of your game. You act like I can't get a man on my own. No, let me rephrase that. You act like I can't even attract a man. Let me assure you right now, that isn't the case."

"Did I say it was?" Dylan asked.

"You didn't have to. It's as plain as the noses on your faces that you're trying to fix me up with somebody. With anybody."

"You've got this all wrong."

"Do I? I think it's you two who have it all wrong, and you need to butt out of my life."

This time it was Luke who spoke. "We're only trying to help, Erin."

"Well, don't," she said. "If I decide I need a man—which I don't—I can find one on my own. Understand?"

"We're concerned. We want to make sure you have someone to take care of you."

Her mouth opened and words came tumbling out. "Take care of me? You both seem to forget that I've been on my own for almost fourteen years. I've traveled the rodeo circuit across this whole country and even into Canada…*by myself.* Nobody was holding my hand. Nobody was keeping me company or taking care of me."

Dylan nodded. "Which is all well and good. But you're older now. Don't you want a family?"

She felt the twinge of regret that always hit her when she thought of what she'd done, nearly seventeen years before. But they didn't know, and she wasn't about to tell them. Ever. She'd had her reasons for staying away from the ranch and for remaining single. And at the age of thirty-four, she wasn't about to get tied down now.

"I *have* a family," she replied. "I have you two. But if you don't stop insisting that I marry the first yahoo that comes along, you'll give me no choice but to leave. Do you understand that?"

Luke looked at Dylan, who shrugged. "You always were stubborn."

"Bullheaded," Luke added.

"No more than the two of you. Shall we talk about your lives before I stepped in to fix them? If it hadn't been for me finding you the perfect women to marry, there's no telling what would have happened to you." She looked pointedly at Dylan, who had come close to losing his share of the ranch, barely a year earlier, until she'd devised a plan to set him up with a former classmate, which had ended in an engagement and an upcoming wedding.

He looked down at her, his green eyes full of a gratefulness she wished he would move beyond. "All right. You've made your point, Erin." He looked at Luke, who nodded, then back at her. "We'll leave you alone, if that's what you want."

She wasn't sure if she should feel relieved. She knew better than to trust them, but they both appeared sincere. "Thank you."

She turned to leave, hoping they wouldn't have to revisit this topic again. The men her brothers had introduced her to had been good men, but she'd never met a man who didn't try to run her life. She suspected she never would.

She didn't mind her solitary life. It was what she'd chosen, and the idea of getting married or anything close to it was out of the question. She liked being single and had no reason to change.

"Fifteen minutes, Erin," Dylan called to her as she started for the door. "No more."

She swallowed her sigh. They weren't going to let her off the hook.

The mere thought of the word *hook* caused her to nearly trip on the threshold. That word reminded her of fishing and ponds and a naked man. A shower was exactly what she needed.

WITHOUT LOOKING, JAKE CANFIELD knew Erin had walked into Lou's Place, Desperation's local tavern. All he'd needed was to hear her voice.

He'd been surprised—no, make that shocked—when he'd spied her lying in the grass near the pond. If he'd known she'd come home, he never would have gone there. Two things had drawn him back. He'd inherited his uncle's ranch, and he'd thought Erin was still on the rodeo circuit. At least he knew now that she wasn't riding. And he was curious to know why. Becoming a barrel racer had always been her dream, much like his own dream of being a rancher. Hers had come true early, and from what he'd heard, she'd done well. Very well. He'd had to wait a while for his, but it had been worth it.

He shouldn't have been surprised to see her at Lou's. After all, she was a grown woman now, not the girl he'd known since he was eight and who'd stolen his heart when he was fifteen.

Had she known it was him at the pond? He hadn't gotten a reply to his question, so he couldn't be sure. He would solve that, though, soon enough.

Turning around, he saw her with her brothers and another man, who at that moment had her hand in his. A pang of jealousy shot through him, and he immediately shook it off. He had no claim on her. All they shared was their childhoods and a night he'd never forgotten. It still hurt to think about it.

He knew the minute she spotted him. Her eyes grew wide, and she took a small, stuttering step back, then quickly regained her composure and nodded in his direction. In reply, he touched the brim of his Stetson. She eased away from her brothers and the man with them, and walked toward him.

She stopped in front of him, and he couldn't hide his smile when she had to tip back her head to look up at him. "I suppose I should have known," she said.

"Good to see you again, too, Erin," he replied. Her hello wasn't as bad as he'd expected.

"Erin?" a woman said from the table behind him.

Erin raised her hand in a wave, but didn't break the gaze that held her to him. "Apparently you've forgotten that Lake Walker is private property. *Walker* property."

"So you did know it was me."

"Not until a minute ago—"

"And you didn't answer my question."

She hesitated for a split second. "What question is that?"

"Did you enjoy the view?"

Her chest rose with a deep breath before she answered, "What *little* I saw wasn't bad."

He had to grit his teeth to keep from laughing. Same old Erin. "I wouldn't use that word, if I were you."

Her eyes narrowed, but the twinkle in them made a lie of it. "What word? *Little?*"

"That would be it. Have you even grown an inch since the last time I saw you?"

She opened her mouth, only to close it. Looking past him, she jerked her thumb in his direction. "You all may have met Jake Canfield, ne'er-do-well, years ago but completely forgot him. It happens a lot."

She'd made her point, and he wished he hadn't mentioned the past. She obviously didn't want to revisit it. Had he hurt her that much?

She flashed him a triumphant smile, and he thought he saw a wink as she walked past him. With a shake of his head and a chuckle, he turned around to see a table where several women were sitting and instantly recognized them from his summers in Desperation.

"That name sounds familiar," one of them

said with a grin, as she offered Jake her hand. "I'm Kate—"

"*Mrs.* Dusty McPherson," Erin finished for her, and looked pointedly at Jake. "You might remember Dusty."

He responded with a smile and took Kate's hand in his. He would play along, if that's what Erin wanted. "I do remember your husband, *Mrs.* McPherson. Quite a bull rider, not long ago. I was sorry to hear he'd retired."

"It's Kate," the woman said, frowning at Erin.

One of the other women from the table leaned in front of Erin, a confused look on her face. "I'm Trish, Kate's sister. Trish Rule."

He released Kate's hand to take Trish's outstretched one. "Sisters, huh?"

"Better behave, Jake. Her husband is the sheriff," Erin announced.

"Is that so? He didn't mention that he had such a pretty wife when I stopped in at his office the other day."

Erin closed her eyes and shook her head, then

moved away. Score one for him. They'd battled on a daily basis, all summer long, every summer he spent at his uncle's ranch. Verbal sparring, he'd called it, and she'd been an expert at it. He learned from her and had gotten pretty good at him himself—until he'd realized she wasn't a little girl anymore and lost his heart to her.

He felt a hand on his back and heard, "Good to see you again, Jake."

Jake turned his head to see Erin's youngest brother. "Luke, it's been a long time. Thanks for returning my dog the other day."

They shook hands as Dylan, the older of the Walker brothers, joined them. "We thought it might be yours, and sorry we missed seeing you. We'd been watching all the building going on at your uncle's place and hoped you had something to do with it."

Jake released Luke's hand to shake his brother's. "Everything to do with it, you could say."

"We were sorry to hear about your uncle," Luke said. "What's it been? Two years?"

Jake nodded. "Close to it. Probate took longer than expected. Seems Uncle Carl owned more than we knew about, most of it on the other side of town. Some in the next county."

"Yeah? I didn't know."

"Neither did I." Jake's mind flashed back to the day he'd received the news that his uncle had died and left the ranch to him, the only nephew. He'd inherited more than he'd ever thought possible and was excited to own his own spread. After turning his back on what his father had wanted him to do, he'd struck out on his own, working for others and learning the ranching business from the bottom up.

"I noticed you and Erin have reconnected," Dylan said, glancing in the direction of his sister, who had taken a seat at the table with Trish and Kate.

"Reconnected?" Jake asked, and chuckled. "More like she was as surprised to see me as

I was to see her. I thought she'd still be barrel racing on the rodeo circuit. Last I knew, she was."

Luke shrugged. "We finally talked her into visiting more often, but never for very long. Then this past February, she pulled in with her motor home and horse trailer, saying she needed a rest."

"With no warning?" Jake asked.

"Not a word," Dylan answered.

"And she's driving us crazy," Luke added. "We're beginning to wish we hadn't encouraged her to come home."

Shaking his head, he smiled. "Sounds like Erin. She still have her horse? Firewind?"

"He's gone. That's all we know," Luke answered. "She has a new one, though. She set up barrels in the spare corral and runs them almost every day."

"But she isn't happy," Dylan said. "She needs something more to do to keep her busy."

Jake didn't doubt he could keep her busy, but

not in the way they were thinking. He hoped her brothers had never learned of what happened that Thanksgiving weekend of his first year in college, when he'd come back to visit. They didn't need to know just how close he and their sister had once been, not to mention how he'd ended it without warning and taken off, never planning to return again.

He shook his head and smiled. "I don't see her taking up knitting any day soon."

Luke laughed. "No kidding."

Dylan glanced at Luke, before saying, "She could use a job."

"Job?"

Luke nodded.

With a glimmer of an idea that might or might not work, he asked, "What kind of job?"

Dylan shrugged. "You know her. When it comes to horses and cattle, there's not much she doesn't know or can't do."

Jake nodded and hoped they'd never know about the things he knew Erin could do.

"From what she's said," Luke continued, "she's spent some of her downtime on her friends' ranches, helping out when needed. She's even worked with some of the ropers, 'refining their skills,' she calls it."

Dylan leaned closer. "Why are you asking?"

It was Jake's turn to shrug. "I just wondered."

"Are you looking for some ranch hands?"

Jake didn't want to commit to anything. The chances of Erin accepting a job from him were slim, at best. Then there was the question of whether he wanted her working for him. There'd be battles. She was strong-minded and could be as stubborn as the day was long. But he couldn't deny that she knew her way around livestock. She would be an asset.

"Maybe," he answered. "Not that she'd take a job on my ranch."

Luke and Dylan looked at each other, and Dylan said, "She might."

Jake was still skeptical.

Luke shook his head. “Don’t worry about it. We understand what a pain she can be.”

Jake didn’t even try to curb his smile. “I guess she never grew out of that.” He was glad she still had the spunk she’d had when they were young. And although he suspected she’d never forgiven him for ending what had barely started, it obviously hadn’t kept her down.

“She has a good heart, though,” Dylan said. “After Pop and Mama died—”

“We appreciated the check you sent to the memorial fund, Jake,” Luke told him. “Your uncle, too.”

Jake nodded. “It was the least we could do. I remember when Uncle Carl called to tell me. I—” He swallowed hard at the memory and how he’d wished he could do something to comfort all of them. David and Ann Walker had treated him like one of their own. “I couldn’t imagine what you all were going through. They were great people.”

Both brothers nodded and were silent for a

moment, and a shadow crossed Dylan's face, before he spoke. "Did you know Erin postponed her rodeo career to stay home with us, until Luke graduated from high school?"

Jake shook his head but wasn't surprised. She'd always been fiercely protective of the two of them. "I didn't know, but that sounds just like her."

"There's nobody like Erin," Dylan said.

After another brief pause, Luke put a hand on Jake's shoulder. "It really is good to see you. We all need to get together again."

"Soon," Jake answered.

"We'll do that. And if you hear anything about a job for someone with Erin's qualifications…"

"I'll pass it on," Jake promised.

As they moved away, he noticed that Erin had left the table where she'd been sitting with the others. After a quick glance around the tavern, he saw her. On the far side of the room, she stood with her hands braced on the old jukebox as she leaned forward to read the list of song titles. He felt a surge of heat shoot through his body but did his best to ignore it. He suspected she wouldn't accept if he approached her about a job. She had a lot of pride, but she had a lot of talent, too. If he hired her it wouldn't be because he wanted to try to repeat the past.

Or did he? He'd never forgotten her. Hardly a day had gone by that he hadn't thought of her. Would it hurt to see if she would take the job? What did he have to lose? He'd already lost her, but maybe he could change that.

ERIN TOOK HER time at the jukebox. She needed to pull herself together. She'd never expected to see Jake Canfield again and wondered if he'd thought the same about her. When she saw him talking with Dusty McPherson and Morgan Rule, she made her way back to the table where Kate and Trish were sitting. She felt light-headed, weak at the knees. She had to stay as far away from Jake as possible until she could regain her equilibrium. Seeing him again had been a shock, and she hadn't felt this vulnerable for a long time. She knew she could handle it, but she wished she didn't have to. She had enough to deal with already.

"You always pick the best music, Erin," Trish said, as she approached the table.

Pulling out the empty chair across from them, Erin settled on it. "There's not a lot to do when you're driving around the country from one place to another."

"And we're so glad you're not doing that anymore and have come home," Kate said.

Even though she'd been home for several months, Erin felt overwhelmed by all the things she still needed to catch up on. "I've missed so much. I guess that's one of the drawbacks of having only brothers. They can rattle off every statistic to do with cattle and crops, but anything else must instantly vaporize in their brains."

"Typical men, then," Trish said, laughing.

"I heard that."

Erin turned and looked up to see Jake, whose frown made deep lines between his gray eyes. In an instant, he revealed the matched set of deep dimples she remembered so well that bracketed his smile. It was that smile and the look in his eyes that could turn her inside out.

She dipped her head to avoid him. She'd known him since she was almost six years old. They'd grown up together. He'd spent summers at his uncle's ranch, and she and her brothers had become friends with him. He'd been tall and thin, a bit gangly and a little on the quiet side. She'd found a hundred ways to make his life hell because of it, and he'd done the same to her.

But the Jake Canfield standing by her now was far from a thin, quiet boy. The image of him in the pond had been burned into her memory as permanently as another memory of him. If she'd known it was him she was watching from the tall grass… She shook her head. She should have known, instead of convincing herself she'd dreamed that he'd spoken to her.

"Right, Erin?"

Lost in thought, she glanced up at him. "Hmm?"

"We were just talking about what a scrawny, ornery tomboy you were when we were growing up."

"No more scrawny than you," she said, but her reply lacked the bite it needed. She had to be careful. If she let him, he would tear her heart out. Again.

But when she saw his steel-colored gaze moving over her as if he knew exactly what she was thinking about, she resolved not to let him break her a second time. Still, it didn't stop the flip-flopping of her heart.

Dusty and Morgan joined them, taking the seats on either side of their wives, and Erin decided it was time to escape. "I think I'll get a snack. Anybody else want something?"

As she started to push her chair back, she felt

Jake's hands on the back of it. "A snack sounds good. I'll go with you."

"Oh, that's all right," she said, standing. "Just tell me what you want, and I'll get it."

His eyebrows shot up, accompanied by a killer smile. "No, that's okay. I don't mind."

Not seeing a graceful way out of it, she nodded. But as soon as they were out of earshot of their friends, she stopped and turned to him. "Are you following me?"

"Could be," he answered, that devilish smile of his reappearing.

"Well, don't."

When she started to walk away, he took her arm and stopped her. "If you'd give me a minute—"

The quick skip of her heart set off warning bells, and her old habits came back. "I think you've had more than a minute with me before." She felt her face grow hot with embarrassment and ducked her head, hoping he didn't notice.

"Can we put the past behind us?" he asked, keeping his voice low.

Hesitating for a moment, unsure of how to answer, she nodded, took a deep breath and looked up. Keep it friendly, she told herself. Pretend none of it happened. "How is the ranching business, Jake?"

"Good. That's what I want to talk to you about."

"Yeah?" She gathered her strength and asked, "Why are you here? You said you weren't coming back. That's what you told me—"

His expression revealed nothing. "I didn't plan to, but Uncle Carl died and left me his ranch."

"Lucky you. Not so lucky for me."

He frowned. "I should've known that's how you'd feel."

The last words he'd said to her, almost eighteen years before, echoed in her mind. "You made your choice."

"I didn't—" He blew out a breath and glanced away. "I had other plans. You knew that."

It hurt, and she didn't want it to. "Not until you told me you were leaving. Not until after we—"

"Erin, it was a long time ago. We were young."

He might as well have stuck a knife in her. "Right. I'd forgotten." She hadn't but wished she could. "Is this what you wanted to talk to me about? Because if it is—"

"No, it isn't. I wanted to talk to you about ranch business." He hesitated and then asked, "How much do you know about cutting horses?"

Taken off guard, she stared at him. "As much if not more than you do. I can rope with the best cowboys around, too. Why?"

Clearing his throat, he glanced around the tavern, then back at her. "I'm looking for somebody to fill an opening at the ranch."

She peered at him through narrowed eyes. "Like who?"

He didn't bother to beat around the bush. "Like you."

Her mouth dropped open and she stared at him. "Me?"

He shrugged. "If you're as good as I suspect you are, yes. I'd like to hire you."

She didn't want to believe him. Work for Jake? Impossible. "Have you suffered some kind of head injury?"

He smiled. "Not recently."

She laughed. "You must be hard up to be offering me a job. If that's what you're doing."

"It's exactly what I'm doing."

She shook her head. "I'm not interested."

She moved away but not far enough to keep from hearing his reply. "Maybe you should think about it."

"Nothing to think about," she answered over her shoulder.

"If you change your mind—"

That stopped her. She took a deep breath and blew it out. Emotions tumbled through her. She needed a job. Money would allow her to get back to barrel racing, where she belonged. But working for Jake? She couldn't.

The last person she wanted to be beholden to—no matter how broke she was, and she was pretty darned broke—was Jake Canfield. Turning to face him, she answered. "Thanks, but—" she broadened her smile and tried for indifference "—I have other plans."

Chapter Two

Jake watched Erin cross the room, a swing in her hips that now had womanly curves. But she was the same Erin. Sassy and headstrong. And she knew horses and cattle. He could use her talents at the ranch, but he'd offered and she'd refused. Why had he even thought she might be interested?

He returned to the table with the others but kept Erin in sight in spite of knowing he shouldn't. Taking his seat, he folded his arms on the table, wondering what he should do next. She obviously considered him the enemy. Too bad he couldn't say the same about her.

Trish reached over and put her hand on his arm. "Next time, try flowers."

"Or dinner at a nice restaurant," Kate added. "Women like that. It gets them out of the kitchen." She frowned at her husband.

Dusty smiled. "You *like* being in the kitchen. You own a bakery and catering business."

"And I like going out—alone with you—once in a while."

"I'll keep that in mind," Dusty said with a grin, then turned to Jake. "Try a rope. It worked for me."

Everyone laughed, causing Jake to wonder what they were talking about. "A rope? Surely you didn't rope this nice lady."

Dusty shrugged one shoulder. "It was the only way to keep her from running away from me."

Jake looked from one to the other. "I have to hear this story."

Leaning back in his chair, Dusty put his arm around his wife. "Let's just say she was resistant to my charm…for too long."

When Kate gave a soft snort, Morgan pointed at Dusty. "He roped her on Main Street on the Fourth of July, in front of the whole town."

"Did you arrest him?" Jake asked the sheriff.

"What for? He wasn't breaking the law."

"I'm telling you," Dusty said, "when you're dealing with a stubborn woman, you do whatever it takes."

Jake smiled. "I'll keep that in mind if I should ever need it. In the meantime, I'll just use simple torture."

Kate's eyes narrowed and the corners of her mouth lifted in a smile. "So it's like that, is it?"

"Nope. Not a bit. But if I didn't give her a hard time, she'd be disappointed and make it tougher on me."

Across the table, Dusty chuckled. "You sure don't want that to happen."

"I was just saying earlier that I was sorry to hear you'd retired from riding," Jake said.

Dusty leaned over to nuzzle his wife's neck.

"She didn't give me a choice. Don't tell her how glad I am that she didn't, though," he added with a wink.

Kate's smug smile pulled a laugh from Jake, but it was clear that the two of them were happy together. He wished he'd had the same luck, but life hadn't worked out that way for him.

He turned to Trish's husband. "How did you manage to end up here in Desperation?"

Morgan chuckled. "I came here from Florida ten years ago to visit my uncle Ernie, and the crazy people in town elected me as their sheriff."

"You've missed a lot," Trish told Jake. "It's been a long time."

Jake caught a glimpse of Erin, who'd pulled up a chair at another table. She sat with her back to him, and he wondered if she'd done so on purpose.

He turned back to the group at his table. "Sounds like a lot has changed in the time I've been gone," he said.

"Are you staying here for good?" Dusty asked.

"I plan to," Jake told him.

"Your uncle's ranch is yours now?"

He nodded, thinking of all the paperwork and court motions it had taken to work out the details of his inheritance.

"What do you plan to do with it?" Dusty asked.

"Raise horses and a few cattle, train cutting and roping horses, mostly. I've learned a lot since those summers I spent here." His dream hadn't happened overnight, but he had stuck with it and now he had it all. Or did he? There was still one thing missing.

He let his gaze wander around the room. Dylan and Luke had gone, leaving Erin behind. If she needed a ride— No, he wouldn't offer. She would only refuse that, too, and he wasn't in the mood to be turned down again.

As the evening grew later, the crowd began to thin. Other people he'd known drifted over to the table to say hello. He enjoyed the company and the evening and looked forward to more of the same in the future.

He liked Desperation. He hadn't spent a lot of time in town when he was young, and yet the people had always been friendly and gone out of their way to make him feel welcome. He'd made friends with several of them and valued those friendships. But the night was nearly over. Even Dusty and Morgan had started talking about going home.

"Kate needs her sleep," Dusty said, putting his arm around her waist when they both stood. "I'm surprised she's managed to stay awake past seven." He placed his other hand on her belly and smiled at her. "Only six more months to go."

Jake saw the look they shared, and then it dawned on him what Dusty had said. "You're expecting?" he asked Kate.

She nodded. "December for this one."

"This one?"

"We have twin boys who'll be three next

month," Dusty said. "And we did tell Aunt Aggie that we wouldn't be late, so we need to get going before she starts calling and begging us to come pick them up."

Kate gave him an elbow to the midsection. "Aunt Aggie has never complained about the boys, or Krista, so don't you have Jake thinking she has."

"I remember your aunt well, Kate," Jake told her. "But who's Krista?"

"Krista is ours," Morgan said, helping his own wife with her chair.

"And we're not adding another one soon," Trish said, a gleam of determination in her eyes. "I have a feeling when we do, Morgan will be getting his boy, and considering how energetic Kate and Dusty's twins are, I want to rest up a little longer."

"Another girl is fine with me," Morgan said, helping her with her jacket. "Krista liked that Miami Dolphins jersey I bought her, so it's all good."

"She was a newborn," Trish said, laughing. "She didn't know the difference."

The two couples continued their bantering as they gathered their things, and Jake was sorry to see them leave. Nearly everyone had gone, except for Erin and the man he'd seen earlier, who was probably taking her home. He decided to stay where he was. He'd noticed that she'd left her hat nearby and knew she wouldn't leave without it.

It wasn't long before she walked over to where he sat at the table, her hat on the chair next to him. "Calling it a night?" he asked.

She didn't look at him directly as she held out her hand. "Morning comes early on a ranch. You should know that."

He shoved to his feet, then picked up her hat, but didn't immediately hand it to her. "What brought you home?"

"I decided to spend some time with my brothers."

"So you're staying around?"

Her gaze moved slowly over him, until she looked directly into his eyes. "Are you?"

Feeling uncomfortable in places he shouldn't, he shifted his attention from her eyes to her mouth. Another mistake. He remembered the feel of it on his far too well. Hoping she couldn't read his thoughts, he managed to answer. "I plan to."

"I should have known."

She took her hat from his hand and started to move away, but he wasn't finished. "Don't go away mad."

With a smile, she looked back over her shoulder. "Not mad. It's just nicer around here when you're gone."

Before she could take another step, he had a comeback. "Is that why you've been gone from here almost as long as I have?"

Facing him, she settled her hat on her head. "I've done just fine."

"So have your brothers, but they stayed." He knew he'd hit the mark by the way she glared at him. "They've done some great things with the ranch."

"So now you and my brothers are good buddies?"

"We've always been friends."

She put one hand on her hip and smiled at him again. "I'm not my brothers."

As she'd done to him, Jake let his eyes move slowly over her. "No, ma'am, you're definitely not." He held her gaze another moment, then looked down to pick up his glass of beer.

When he looked up again, she was walking out the door. Walking out on him the way he'd walked out on her. He knew she hadn't forgotten, no matter how much she might want to. He'd hated that he'd had to hurt her—still did—but he hadn't been given a choice. He'd paid for it then, and now he was paying for it again.

AFTER A DISTURBING and restless night, Erin decided to join her brothers for breakfast. In her case, that would be coffee. She hoped it would clear her mind and sweep out the remnants of the confusing and erotic dreams that had starred none other than Jake Canfield.

"Did you have a good time at Lou's Place last night?" Luke asked, as Erin lifted the carafe to fill her cup.

When she finished, she leaned her hip against the counter behind her and nodded. "It was nice getting together with old friends, but it would have been better if Hayley and Glory had been there and the two of you hadn't ducked out. What was that all about?"

"We didn't tell you we weren't staying?"

She glared at Luke, knowing for certain what they'd been up to. "Of course you didn't tell me, because you knew I wouldn't go if you did. And then you left me with that…man."

"You mean Dean Franklin?"

She opened her mouth to tell him that Dean Franklin had been kind enough to take her home, in spite of the fact that she'd only spent a few minutes with him, and that the man she'd been referring to was none other than their former—and now current—neighbor. Luckily, the words didn't spill forth. Her brothers would immediately demand to know what Jake had ever done to her, other than be a good friend, and she wouldn't be able to tell them. Not in this lifetime, anyway.

Instead, she said, "Maybe you'll learn not to try to hand me off to someone I share absolutely nothing in common with."

"Broaden your world, Erin. Learn new things," Dylan told her.

"The man wouldn't know a quarter horse from a thoroughbred," she said with a sniff, "and you expect me to make some long-term commitment to him?"

Dylan put his coffee cup on the table and grunted. "Nobody said you had to marry him. Just go on a date."

"People still date?" she asked as innocently as possible.

"Well—"

"Did you take Glory on a date?" she asked, pinning him with a look she hoped would wither him on the spot.

His brow wrinkled in thought. "We—" He made a face she took as a concession. "Not a real date. But that doesn't mean that—"

"How about you and Hayley, Luke? Did you go on a date?"

He smiled with superiority. "As a matter of fact, I did take her out to dinner. A real nice restaurant in the city, as I recall."

"How did it go?"

His smile vanished, and he muttered.

"What's that?" she asked.

"She got sick."

Erin couldn't stop her smile. "Food poisoning?"

He shook his head. "Too much to drink."

"Well, there you go."

They both sat and stared at her, until Dylan

pushed away from the table. "What's on your agenda today?"

When Luke didn't answer, Erin looked at Dylan. "Me? Are you asking me?"

"I already know what our plans are."

He'd said it as if she was twelve again and he was trying to prove that bigger meant smarter. It didn't. Being only eleven months older than him gave her an advantage.

"Nothing special," she answered. Her lack of having something to do was beginning to get on her nerves. She'd always been self-sufficient and kept busy, and she couldn't tell them that she was as broke as anyone could get without being completely homeless. Between entry fees and living expenses, with money going out faster than it had come in, she'd had to take a break, regroup and hoped to find a way to earn enough money to get back on track. But she wouldn't take a penny from her brothers.

"You need to do something," Dylan said.

What she needed was a job, but the only

offer she'd had was from a man who'd broken her heart. She quickly searched for something to say. "I thought I might drop in at Glory's shop later and see if there's anything I can help with."

"She's at the Big Barn at the Commune, finishing the last of the painting." Dylan got to his feet and looked down at her. "She probably wouldn't mind if you stopped by. I'm sure she could use some help."

Erin nodded but didn't commit herself. She really liked her brothers' fiancées and hoped they would become good friends. But that would probably come later, when she didn't feel as if she were living in some kind of limbo.

Luke had left the table and joined Dylan at the door, where they both grabbed their hats from the rack on the wall. "We'll be down at the barn, in case you need anything."

She told them goodbye and waited until they were gone, then closed her eyes and let out a long sigh. Going into town for her own coffee to make in her motor home would solve the problem of feeling useless. At least it was something to do.

Two cups later, she was out the door and headed for her motor home, thinking she'd make a list of groceries she should get. It wouldn't be much, but enough to get her by, until she had a job. Even though she'd asked everywhere she thought might be hiring—even the day care center that was run by a friend of a friend—she'd come up empty-handed.

She wasn't particularly looking forward to a trip into town. Driving her gas-guzzling home-on-wheels in Desperation had proved cumbersome, at best, but unless she borrowed Dylan's pickup, she was stuck driving it. The thought didn't thrill her.

As she reached for the door handle of her small but comfortable home, she stopped at the sound of something rustling in the nearby line of trees. Maybe a rabbit. Probably a skunk, with her luck. Hopefully not anything bigger. Her shotgun was inside in the back of a cabinet.

She immediately saw she'd been wrong, when the big, hairy dog pushed through the undergrowth and shot into the open. "Well, hello," she called softly, being cautious so as not to frighten it.

The dog froze when she spoke. Its long, gray-and-white coat nearly reached the ground. Even its eyes were partially hidden. Lifting its nose higher, it sniffed in her direction.

Hoping the dog wouldn't bite, she snapped her fingers and called again. "Come on, pup. Come here. Let's see what you're about."

She barely had the words out of her mouth, when the dog came running toward her, its furry tail wagging back and forth. Bracing herself for what she suspected might be a lunge—although a friendly one—that would knock her over, she was surprised when the dog came to a skid in front of her, all four feet still on the ground. Most dogs would jump up. This one obviously had some training.

Kneeling, she put her hand on the back of the dog's neck, feeling for a collar. "Good dog," she whispered. "Now let me see if you have a tag or some kind of identification to go with this."

She was rewarded with a tag dangling beneath the dog's neck but had to brush away the thick, long coat of hair to see it. "Solomon?" She leaned back to take a closer look at the dog. "Is that your name?"

The dog's tail wagged so hard when she spoke the name that she had no doubt it was his. But she couldn't find a phone number or anything else that would give her an idea of who the owner might be. Solomon appeared to be well fed and fairly clean, considering the thick brush he'd walked through, and he'd probably come from somewhere nearby.

"Let's go talk to my brothers," she said, getting to her feet. "Come on, Solomon. Stick with me, and we'll get you home in no time."

He walked beside her to the barn, where she found her brothers helping with the birth of a new calf. Luke looked up as Erin and the dog entered, and he shook his head. "Sollie, are you out visiting again?"

"So you know who his owner is?" she asked, relieved that the dog wasn't a stray. "Should I call someone?"

Dylan glanced at them quickly. "No. Just take him home."

"Take him home where?"

"Sollie belongs to Jake."

She narrowed her eyes and looked at the dog. *Traitor.* Even though her brothers were working, she didn't want to deal with the dog…and especially his owner. "Why can't I leave him here with you?" she asked. "Jake can come get his own dog."

"Just take him home, Erin," Dylan said without glancing her way again. “Can’t you see we have our hands full?”

“Of course I do. Can I take your pickup? I don’t want him in my motor home.”

“Walk.”

She started to ask why, but it was clear Dylan’s patience was wearing thin. This obviously wasn’t the first time the dog had come visiting, and her brothers had taken him home. That meant they’d known Jake was back. Why hadn’t they mentioned it?

“Let’s go, Sollie,” she said, heading outside and blinking at the bright sunlight.

The walk wasn’t as long as she wanted to make it out to be, and the dog stayed by her side. At one point, not far from the ranch that Jake now owned, Sollie came to a dead stop, sniffing the air, his ears on alert.

“It’s a rabbit, I’m sure,” she told the dog. “We’re almost home, so don’t you go running off after it.”

As if he understood what she’d said, Solomon loped along beside her, but now and then he would look off in the distance. She was surprised that anything that had been around Jake could be so well behaved.

Approaching the ranch from the back side, as she'd always done, she spied Jake on a small tractor with a forklift attached to the front, struggling to move a large stock tank. As she and the dog got closer, she heard the frustration in Jake's voice, and she laughed at the words he shouted at the galvanized metal tank that kept tipping to one side. She understood frustration well. She'd bought an extra horse, hoping to train it to be as good as Firewind. But she'd had to have Firewind put down, and MacDuff's training hadn't gone well. Just one more reason she'd left the circuit.

"Get under it again," she shouted over the noise from the tractor. "A little more to the right."

Apparently he heard her, because he turned to look in their direction. He shook his head as if in disbelief, and then switched off the tractor before jumping down to the ground.

"Sollie, you rascal," he said as he walked toward them, his mouth pulled down in a frown. He glanced at Erin, but his gaze didn't linger. "Sorry he caused you the trouble of bringing him home. He knows better than to roam."

She ran her hand down the dog's back and patted his rump. "He's a good dog. Smart, too."

"Too smart sometimes. I guess I'll have to tie him up when I'm working so he doesn't bother you."

"Oh, don't do that!" She bit her lower lip, wishing she'd kept quiet. It wasn't any of her business what he did with his dog. Besides, she wasn't crazy about the idea of having to return Sollie after every visit. "He wasn't bothering me," she hurried to say. "I brought him back because I thought you'd wonder where he'd gone."

"I had a pretty good idea."

"What kind of dog is he?"

"He's a bearded collie. Herding dog, both sheep and cattle. He's pretty good at it."

She nodded, not knowing what else to say. Wishing she had insisted her brothers return the dog themselves, she took a step back and realized she'd just met up with her past. If she'd thought there'd been too many memories at home, a single memory of one night here was even bigger than all of them.

"I guess I'll be getting home," she said, feeling uncomfortable.

"Hang on a minute."

She slowed, then stopped and looked back at him. "Why?"

He stuffed his hands into the pockets of a pair of well-worn jeans that hugged his hips and muscled thighs. No smile broke the serious expression on his face, when he said, "Because we need to talk."

Her heart stopped beating and her throat tightened. The moment she'd realized he was back, she'd been afraid he would want to talk about the past. The words *fight or flight* flitted through her mind, but she was frozen to the spot.

JAKE SQUINTED INTO the morning sunshine, watching Erin closely. Her curly, dark blond hair had been captured in a braid, but pieces of it had escaped around her face, and the sun behind her caused a halo effect.

This was the first chance he'd had to get a good look at her. The day before, the tree at the pond had cast shadows on her sleeping form—if she'd actually been asleep. And the tavern last night hadn't provided the best lighting, either. But now he didn't miss how pale she'd become when he'd mentioned they needed to talk.

He knew he'd hurt her in the past, but he'd hoped that time might have taken care of that. He'd been young, although not as young as she'd been, and he hadn't had a choice. Sooner or later she would have gotten hurt, and he'd believed at the time that sooner would be better.

He wasn't some kind of ogre, out to break her heart again. He really did need the help that she was more than qualified to give. And he suspected she could use the money. He could help her with that, and in turn she would be helping him. Sleep had evaded him for most of the night, as he'd thought about his long-ago dream of them working side by side at a ranch. It could come true now. Even if it was only as employer-employee, it would be something.

But he also knew he had to tread carefully. "I apologize for Sollie causing trouble. If it happens again, give me a call, and I'll pick him up."

She avoided looking directly at him. "It's not a problem. I—I don't get enough exercise as it is, so he did me a favor."

Sollie had done them both a favor by getting her on his territory. Now he had the advantage.

"Not exactly the kind of exercise you're used to, but it's always good to stay active."

She nodded, shifting from one foot to the other. "The boys talked me into coming home more often, and here I am."

He knew she meant her brothers. The Walkers had always been a close family. "How long do you plan to stay?"

"I haven't decided."

It was his turn to nod, and he thought hard about what he could say next that would keep her there long enough for him to repeat his job offer. She might turn it down again, but if he could calm her nerves first, she just might consider it.

Then he remembered what Luke had said about her horse. "What happened to Firewind?"

She lowered her head. "He had to be put down."

Jake felt a heaviness in his chest. He could only imagine what that had done to her. She'd loved that horse. The two of them had won events across the country. He still remembered the day she'd gotten him for her fourteenth birthday.

"I'm sorry, Erin. I know how much he meant to you. Was he sick?"

Without looking up, she shook her head. "Just old. Tired and worn out. Putting him down was the kindest and best thing to do for him."

Every cell in his body urged him to take the few steps needed to pull her into his arms and comfort her. But he knew it would be wrong. Instead, he simply said, "It's a hard thing to do."

Slowly lifting her head, she met his gaze. "I've been training another horse. It's slow going, though." She breathed a tired sigh. "We haven't connected the way Firewind and I did."

"It can take time. Do you miss him?"

A sad smile lifted one corner of her mouth. "Every day."

She'd relaxed some, but he wasn't quite ready

to bring up the job yet. "You always had a good eye when it came to horses."

Looking down again, she shrugged, as if the praise embarrassed her. "Maybe. But I must've misjudged with Lord MacDuff."

Jake chuckled at the name. "Do you call him Lord or Your Grace?"

She glanced at him, wrinkling her nose. "Neither. It's MacDuff, and His Grace is questionable."

So she'd taken a break because her horse didn't respond the way she needed it to. That would have made sense to him, *if* she had been anyone else. When it came to animals, Erin had a gift that few people possessed. Sollie had obviously taken to her immediately, and he wasn't always that way with strangers. Horses, though, had always been her specialty. Maybe she'd misjudged this new horse because she'd been mourning Firewind, and that had brought on a lack of belief in herself.

Would working with other horses help? He

was willing to let her try…if she was. "Have you worked with other horses?"

She tilted her head to one side. "Since Firewind?" she asked, and he nodded. "Some."

"How did it go?"

"Good."

Hope sank its hooks into him, and he had to hold back a smile. "No problems? They responded to you well?"

"Yes, very well, in fact."

"Maybe working with a few more horses would give you some distance and then working with MacDuff would go better." He waited, watching her press her lips together.

"I suppose it could," she finally said. "But—"

"I have plenty of horses here you could work with. In fact, the ranch needs someone like you." He'd made sure he hadn't said that *he* needed her. "With your talent…"

He knew the instant she realized what he was doing and was certain he'd blown his chance.

She tugged at her ear as if weighing the

pros and cons of working for him, then looked him square in the eye. "You pay pretty well, right?"

He searched for the right words, knowing he couldn't push. "No one's complained."

"Cutting horses and roping?"

His heart beat faster. This might work, after all. "Yeah."

"You're offering me a job. Again."

Hoping he didn't sound desperate, he answered, "I am."

Seconds that seemed like hours ticked by as a range of emotions moved across her face. Indecision, apprehension and then capitulation. "All right," she said. "I'll take it."

He looked down, fighting a smile of victory. When he had it under control, he looked up. "You're sure?"

She locked her gaze with his, determination turning her blue-green eyes darker. "I'm sure."

Nodding, he allowed a small smile. "Welcome to the team, then. When can you start?"

"Whenever you want me."

His imagination ran wild, but he kept a straight face. "Is that so?"

She seemed to be fighting a snappy comeback and then sobered. "There's just one thing."

"What's that?" he asked, shoving lusty images from his mind.

"Treat me the same as you do the other wranglers."

This time, he didn't try to hide his smile. "You mean we shouldn't be intimate friends?"

She drew herself up and looked him in the eye. "Don't start, Jake, or I'm gone."

Ready to agree to just about anything, he dipped his head in a quick nod. "Whatever you say."

After telling Sollie goodbye, while pointedly avoiding making eye contact with Jake, she turned for home.

"Monday morning, eight o'clock," he called to her. "And don't be late."

She waved a hand without looking back and kept going.

He watched her, hardly believing she'd accepted. He'd won. But how long would his victory last? Only time would tell, and he had plenty of that.

Chapter Three

Erin's boots felt as if they were filled with cement as she walked across the neighboring pastures to the Morris ranch. Or the Canfield ranch, she corrected, since it now belonged to Jake, Carl Morris's nephew. By Saturday night, after she'd told Jake she would work for him, she'd come to the conclusion that she'd made a dangerous error by accepting the job he'd offered her. Sunday found her feeling fifty-fifty about it, with half her time spent reminding herself that she hadn't found work anywhere else and this was the best she could do for the time being. The other half had been spent wondering if she'd lost her mind. By this morning, when her alarm went off, she'd come to the point of not caring. She had a job. One she might even enjoy, in spite of her employer.

Now that she was halfway to the ranch, her nerves had stretched as tight as a size eight girdle on an elephant. She *was* crazy. Work for Jake? He'd always been her biggest weakness. She'd thought she'd outgrown that, but apparently she hadn't. Nonetheless, it wouldn't stop her from doing the best job she could, if only to prove to Jake that she was even better than he thought.

As she approached the ranch, she could see the other cowboys arriving. What would they think of working with a woman? Her apprehension grew with each step she took, until she found herself at the edge of the largest of the corrals, behind an obviously new barn. To the right of it was the sprawling two-story house with the wraparound porch, where Jake had spent his summers. Without thinking, her gaze moved beyond it to the big gambrel-roof barn that held the memory she'd put behind her. Or tried to. Everything that happened after that, except the accident that had taken her parents' lives, had been affected by the decision she'd made that night he'd come back from college.

She took a deep breath and looked away to see several smaller, new corrals encircling the large ranch yard—strong indications that he planned to stay. If she gained nothing else from this crazy need to prove she could be strong and face down anything thrown at her—including working for Jake—at least she would earn the money she needed. He obviously had plenty.

Lost in her thoughts, she nearly jumped out of her boots when she heard him say her name. Slapping her hand over her suddenly racing heart, she spun around to find him standing only a few feet away.

"You made it," he said, a hint of surprise in his gray eyes.

Proof, she thought, that he'd expected she

wouldn't show up. "Of course I did. Why wouldn't I?"

"No reason."

He looked her over from top to bottom and back again, sending a warm flush through her, until her clenched teeth made her jaw ache. No one could affect her the way Jake did, and she wished he would stop.

"Come meet the others," he said, turning around and leaving her to cool down and collect her wits.

She nearly had to run to keep up with his long strides. Ahead of them, she saw the other ranch hands greeting each other. "Is this all of us?" she asked. "Three men and me?"

"For now, it is. I could use one more. Maybe two," he answered. "As the ranch grows, so will the crew."

Impressed, she had to smile. "That business degree is paying off."

They'd almost reached the others when he

stopped and looked down at her. "There's no degree."

When he moved on, she stumbled as she hurried to catch up with him, her mind stuttering on what he'd said. "Why not?" she asked, curious why he hadn't finished the college degree he'd seemed to want so badly. Badly enough to leave her behind.

"Why not what?" he asked, keeping his attention straight ahead.

"Why don't you have that degree?"

Several steps later, he answered. "I quit school in the second semester of my sophomore year."

This time she didn't stumble. She came to a stop, unable to take another step. *He quit school?* But before she could say it aloud, he'd joined the others and stood waiting for her.

"Erin, these are your coworkers. That's Bobby Ray," Jake said, pointing to a tall, lean, forty-something cowboy, who tipped the brim of his hat with his finger.

"Ma'am," he drawled.

"Hello, Bobby Ray."

Jake barely gave her a glance, his focus on his employees. "That over there's Gary. We've worked together for several years. And this here's Kelly, our most recent employee."

And the youngest, she thought. Mid-twenties, she guessed when Kelly smiled at her. Gary was close to Jake's age, in his mid-thirties, with light blue eyes framed by deep crinkles at the corners.

"This is Erin Walker, boys," Jake finished. "And before you think there isn't a whole lot to her, I can assure you she not only knows what she's doing, she's a lot tougher than she looks."

"It's nice to meet you all," Erin said, looking at each of them.

Before any of them spoke, Jake issued duties for the morning. The men hurried off to do their work, and he turned back to her. "Think you can handle it?"

"I don't see why not." None of the other hands had made her feel out of place, although she sensed they weren't sure what to think of her. Not a new reaction. She'd lived most of her life in a man's world, and it happened regularly. "I'm pretty sure that if you hired them, they know what they're doing."

"They do," he answered.

"So what's my job? What is it, exactly, that I've been hired to do?"

"We'll talk about that later. After you've had a chance to see the operation, we can decide. Until then, why don't you go observe each of them? You have a good eye, and I'd be interested to hear what you think."

She noticed he'd said "we can decide" instead of "I will decide" and was surprised. Deep down, she knew she shouldn't be. When they were growing up, he'd always shown interest in her riding and had constantly asked her and her brothers questions about horses, livestock and ranching in general.

"I can do that," she answered, only a little nervous that she would be observing, not working, at least for now. "In the meantime, I look forward to getting to know my fellow employees."

That brought a smile from him. "Just treating you like the others."

"Thanks."

He moved away, and then stopped. "If you have any questions, let me know. I have some other things to take care of, but I'll be around."

When he headed in the direction of the big barn where she'd seen Kelly disappear, she blew out a breath. So far, so good.

For the next few hours, she watched the other wranglers, making mental notes of how they handled the animals and of their strengths and weaknesses. What that had to do with the job she would be assigned, she didn't know. But she guessed Jake would tell her before the day ended.

Leaning against the corral fence, she felt someone walk up behind her and she turned to see the object of her thoughts.

"How's it going?" he asked.

"Good. Not that I know why I'm doing it, but you're the boss."

"You always were a fast learner."

No way would she answer that. She couldn't be sure what he was referring to, but it was better that she didn't try to guess.

He must have picked up on what she was thinking, because she caught a ghost of a smile on his lips before he spoke. "What do you think of them?"

"As a whole?"

"Yeah."

"They seem to get along with each other," she said. "There aren't any slackers, so nobody is forced to do anyone else's job. They each do their own thing, but they seem friendly toward each other. It's a good group, at least from what I've seen."

"And individually?"

She didn't know how to answer. "Do you want an honest assessment?"

"Nothing but."

Nodding, she glanced around the big ranch yard, where the men continued working with the livestock and focused on what they were doing, not on Jake. "Bobby Ray is good. It's easy to see that he has a lot of experience. But I also see a little weakness in his roping."

"All right. Go on."

"Gary seems to know what he's doing and is doing it right. At least that's my observation."

"I expect that."

He wasn't giving her much to go on, but she continued. "I didn't see much of Kelly."

"Kelly's helping me with some updates in the barn."

"Have you given any thought to hiring a few high school boys to help with those kinds of things?"

"No, I haven't. Should I?"

He was being far too reasonable and it made her nervous. "Glory hired a few last year to help with work on the house."

"I'll think about it."

She waited for him to say more, and when he didn't, she looked up at him. It was the wrong thing to do. He was watching her closely, his eyes smoky and half-lidded. She knew that look all too well. It had always made her feel as if her bones were turning to liquid. It still did.

She needed to get away, have a little time to herself. Thirty minutes. An hour, at the most. But how?

He blinked, clearing his eyes, and stepped back. "Lunch is at noon."

Her knees weakened at the reprieve. "I'll go home for that," she answered, with effort. "What time do I need to be back?"

"We all go to the café. Together."

So much for getting a little time to herself to put some space between them. But she'd insisted on being treated as one of them, so she couldn't complain now.

JAKE STUDIED THE ice in his glass of tea, wondering if he'd done the right thing by hiring Erin.

The five of them were nearly finished with their lunch at the Chick-a-Lick Café. He'd noticed immediately when Erin chose the seat farthest away from him. She'd even insisted on sitting in the backseat of his crew cab pickup on the way into town. He reminded himself that this was only the first day. There would be plenty of time to fix things between them.

He heard her laugh and moved his chair a little more to the left, hoping to get a better view of her. As he did, Darla, their waitress and the café manager, placed the bill next to him. He looked up with a smile. "Great meal, as always, Darla," he told her.

"Thanks, Jake," she replied, and then turned to look down the table. "It's good to see you again, Erin," she said with a friendly smile. "You probably don't remember me. I was finishing eighth grade when you graduated from high school."

"Of course I remember you," Erin answered. "You have three brothers. Patrick was in my class."

Darla's smile widened. "Yes, he was."

"What's he doing?"

"He moved to the city. He's a doctor. My mother is thrilled."

Erin laughed, and Jake wished she would laugh at something he said. She'd spent the morning staying out of his range, and he'd played it smart by keeping his distance, as much as possible.

"Eat up, boys," he said, purposely not mentioning Erin's name. After all, she wanted to be treated like them. "We need to be getting back soon."

"Well, I'll be danged!"

Jake looked down the table at Bobby Ray, sitting across the table from Erin and staring at her.

"I knew there was something about you," Bobby Ray continued, "but I couldn't put my finger on it. It just came to me like a lightning bolt. You're Erin Walker."

Putting her glass aside, she leaned back and

crossed her arms, her face calm and straight. "That's my name."

Bobby Ray glanced at Jake, who smiled. He had an idea where this was going and knew it would be interesting.

Shaking his head, Bobby Ray leaned forward. "No. I mean yes, you are, but I mean *the* Erin Walker, the barrel racer. I've seen you compete."

She didn't say anything at first, then spoke directly to him. "Did you rodeo, Bobby Ray?"

His nod was short and quick. "I did, back in the day. Team roping. By the time I really got the hang of it, the younger cowboys were catching up. I decided it must not be for me."

"He's not being honest," Jake said, from his end of the table. "He and his partner won several competitions."

Bobby Ray shook his head. "Not enough to keep me in it. It's a tough life. And an expensive one, if you aren't on the winning side more than the losing."

Erin didn't respond at first, leaving Jake to wonder what was going through her head.

"It takes more than talent," she finally said, giving Bobby Ray a smile Jake wished she'd bestowed on him.

"Well, you've got that, for sure," the wrangler answered.

"What's it like, Erin?" Kelly asked. "Traveling around the country."

She gave a little one-shouldered shrug. "It's like living life as a gypsy. Sometimes exciting. Sometimes just a lot of driving. This is such a beautiful country, and I've been lucky to see so much of it. But the rodeo circuit, like everything else, has its ups and downs, pros and cons."

Jake had never thought her life had been easy, but this was the first time, except for when she'd talked about Firewind, that he'd caught a note of loneliness in her voice. Most of the time it was spit and fire. The years had changed her, at least a little.

Standing, he announced, “We’d better be getting back.”

The others started moving, and while he walked on to the cash register, they left the café. When he finished paying the bill, he found them waiting on the sidewalk in front of his truck and joined them.

“Maybe Erin should sit in front, this time,” Gary said, opening the front passenger door.

“I’m fine in the back,” she answered quickly. “You and Jake need the extra leg room.”

“Less crowded with you in the front,” Jake pointed out.

“Maybe another time,” she said, without looking at him.

His gaze lingered on her for a moment, and then he walked around the front of the truck and climbed in. “Let’s get a move on, boys.”

They’d reached the outskirts of town when Bobby Ray leaned forward. “Were you going to look into that cattle sale down in Wichita Falls?”

"I plan to," Jake answered.

"I hear they'll have some nice horses, too."

"It's two weeks away, so I'll check into that more closely before I go. Can't have too many horses," Jake said, and glanced in the rearview mirror. Erin didn't seem to hear him as she stared out the window. If only he knew what she was thinking. Or maybe it was best that he didn't.

The rest of the ride back to the ranch remained quiet. As he turned the truck into the ranch yard, he tried to think of something he could have Erin do that would keep her nearby.

He'd just gotten out of the truck and closed the door, when he saw her catching up with Bobby Ray, heading for the large corral. The nearly windless day helped carry her voice, so he watched and listened.

"I noticed you were having a little trouble this morning, Bobby Ray," she said, matching his stride.

"Slow reaction speed," he answered.

"I think we can fix that."

He turned his head to look at her. "You think so?"

"Yeah, I do. Would you mind if I gave you a few tips? I learned a lot doing ranch work during breaks."

He stopped, still looking at her, and Jake waited. Bobby Ray was a good ol' boy, and Jake wasn't sure how the cowboy might take her offer.

"You'd do that?" Bobby Ray asked.

"Only if you want me to," she answered.

He pulled off his battered cowboy hat and scratched his head. "Well, now, ma'am, I can't say it would hurt me, if you know what I mean."

"We all started at the beginning and had to learn," Erin said. "Sometimes more than once."

"That's the truth." He replaced his hat and then offered her his arm. "I'd be honored if you'd give me some tips on what will make my ropin' better, Miz Walker."

Her smile was bright, and she looped her arm through his. "Then let's get to it. And it's *Erin*."

Jake watched them enter the corral and thought again about what she'd said at the café. He'd followed her career for many years and knew she'd had several good wins, almost making it to the National Finals a few times. But he also knew it took money to get from rodeo to rodeo. Considering the cost of gas, entry fees, food, feed and vet care for her horse, and everything else, it could get expensive. Was that why she'd come home? She'd admitted that her new horse was in need of more training. If she hadn't been winning and had paid out more than she'd won, it made sense that she'd left. The question now was whether she intended to return to her rodeo life or if she'd left it behind and wanted to move on to something else.

He didn't know if he wanted to hear the answer. When he did, maybe he would ask her.

Until then, he would wait and see how things worked out—or didn't work out—between them.

At quitting time, he stood in the yard, praising his men for a good day as they climbed into their vehicles. When they started their engines and began to drive away, he noticed that Erin had already started for home.

"Can I give you a ride?" he called to her.

Facing him, she walked backward and kept going. "I don't mind the walk, but thank you."

When she turned back, he lengthened his stride, catching up with her, before she'd gone too far. "More exercise?" he asked, stepping up to walk beside her.

"It can't hurt."

"You look fine to me." As soon as it was out of his mouth, he regretted saying it and was thankful she didn't have a quick comeback. "It was nice what you did with Bobby Ray today."

"He strikes me as a good man," she said, glancing up at him. "The talent is there. He just needs a little practice on some of the things I showed him."

"You didn't have to do that."

She stopped. "Isn't that why you hired me?"

"Sure. Some of it." He wouldn't tell her that he'd also had personal reasons. Very personal. She would figure that out on her own, soon enough.

"Then there's no need to talk about it," she said, then hesitated. "All you have to do is tell me the job you want me to do, and I'll do the best I can. That's how I work."

He knew that. She'd been born into ranching—one big reason he'd hired her. But he'd worked hard at it. Spent years on other people's ranches, starting at the bottom. Things were different now. He was the boss. He just hadn't adjusted to it yet.

"It's only your first day."

She shifted from one foot to the other. "And I can't keep wandering around, watching others. I need to work with the rest of them. It's pretty clear you need me, or at least someone. And it wouldn't hurt to hire another person, especially if you plan to add more livestock."

He couldn't argue with that, but it wasn't as easy as she might think. He'd worked with Gary, so that had been easy. He'd found Bobby Ray through a friend, and Kelly had answered an ad.

"I intend to. There's a flyer in the café, and I put ads in several ranching papers and magazines," he explained. "It doesn't happen overnight. Not with experienced men."

She nodded but didn't say anything.

When he heard a bark, he turned to see his dog and welcomed the interruption. "Looks like Sollie's coming to tell you goodbye."

"Tell him I'll see him tomorrow." When she walked away, she moved fast.

"Same time in the morning," he shouted as she gained ground.

She waved at him, without looking back.

Sollie stopped beside him, giving his hand a

nudge. "Yeah, she's gone for the day. But she'll be back." Scratching Sollie's head, he watched her until she disappeared from his sight. He looked down at the dog. "We have to keep her here, Sollie. I know you don't understand, but we have to."

JONAH BUTTERFIELD WINCED at the beginnings of a blister on his heel, inside his nearly new boots. He'd done more walking in the past day than he had in half of his almost seventeen years. He hadn't, really. It only felt as though he had. But it didn't matter. He was on a mission.

Kicking up dust from the shoulder of the road, he looked again to see if the ranch he needed to find was close by. No house, yet, but he did spy a large, country mailbox set on a post and hoped his journey might be nearing its end.

Another dozen steps, and he could make out the name on the mailbox. JAKE CANFIELD, it said, in bright blue letters. He'd finally made it to his destination, and with nothing but the name of a town, some initials and that name.

He reached the box and stood staring at it for several seconds. No one knew him or knew why he was there. They would learn soon enough.

Taking a deep breath, he started up the long drive to a large two-story house. Nice. Not some old place like a few he'd seen. Behind it were what looked like a couple of barns and some white fences. Corrals. He'd seen them in pictures.

As he walked closer, he saw two cowboys, each leading a horse. He needed to find the one who owned the ranch.

No one seemed to notice him, so he had a chance to run through what he planned to say. He would just tell them he'd been traveling through on the way to visit a friend and stopped at the café in town, where he'd seen a help-wanted flyer. Not exactly the truth, but good enough. He *had* seen the flyer, but he'd already known to look for a guy named Jake at the Canfield ranch. That much he'd learned while thumbing through a ranching magazine at the library.

He felt pretty safe. No one would be looking for him yet. In a day or two, maybe, but he had some—

"Hey, kid."

Jonah looked to his right and saw a sandy-haired man walking toward him. "Mr. Canfield?" he asked, hoping he had the right guy.

"Hang on," the man said, and turned around. "Hey, Jake! Somebody's here looking for you."

"Send him over," the man who answered to the name said.

So that was him, Jonah thought, as he thanked the first guy and walked over to where Jake stood talking to a woman. A cowgirl, he guessed, by the jeans, boots and hat. Jake's wife?

"Mr. Canfield?" he asked again.

The guy looked at him. "Yeah, that's me."

No turning back now. “A man gave me a ride—”

“Are you here about the job?”

How lucky could a guy get? He didn’t even have to ask or anything. But he would have to wing the rest of it. He hadn’t thought much beyond this. “Yeah. Could you use another hand?”

The woman next to him started to move away, but Jake stopped her. “Stay. We’re not through.” Then he turned back to Jonah. “What’s your name?”

“Jonah. Jonah Butterfield.”

“How old are you, Jonah?”

“Eighteen, sir.” Okay, that was a stretch, but did it matter?

Jake looked him over. “You have identification?”

Heart plummeting, Jonah reached around to his back pocket, juggling the backpack he wore, while keeping a tight grip on his duffel bag. “Right here.”

“No, that’s okay,” Jake said, stopping him.

"I can get that later. How much do you know about horses?"

"Not a whole lot," Jonah answered, truthfully this time. "But I'm willing to learn." When Jake started to shake his head, Jonah hurried on. "I'm a quick learner." Even his dad said so, not that he cared what his dad said.

Jake glanced at the woman, who shrugged, and then he asked another question. "Do you live around here, Jonah?"

"No, sir. Up north."

Jake looked at him, his eyes squinting a little. "Where, exactly, would that be?"

Jonah hoped he didn't have to get too specific, or the whole thing might blow up. He wasn't ready to walk away, not until he found who he'd set out to look for, got a few questions answered and then said what he'd come to say.

"I'm from Kansas," he answered.

The woman took a small step back but didn't say anything. He pretended he didn't notice, but then she pinned him in place with a look that would have frozen anyone with half a brain.

"How was it again that you learned about the job?" She added a smile that made her look less threatening.

This he could handle. He had it all figured out, and it wasn't all that far from the truth. He answered her smile with his own, but turned to Jake. He knew who the boss was, and it wasn't her.

"I've been looking for a job," he began, "and saw the notice in a ranching magazine and thought since it's not all that far from home—you know, like thousands of miles," he added, "it would be a good start."

He saw the look Jake gave the woman, like she didn't really have any business asking. Maybe it wasn't his wife, after all.

Jake rubbed his hand along his jaw and squinted as if he was thinking hard on it. "So you really want to be a wrangler?" he asked.

"It's all I've been thinking about for a long time, and—"

"Come on, Jake," the woman said. "It takes time to teach a kid."

Jake looked at her. "Maybe you should be the one to do it, then."

Her chin went up and she squinted her eyes to look up at him. "I have enough to do."

"Is that right?"

"If you want these horses trained, I do."

Jonah had to choke back a laugh. They would have been nose to nose, if she hadn't been so much shorter than Jake. Whoever she was, she wasn't afraid of the guy, that was for sure.

"You're the best one to teach him," Jake said, his voice a little lower and softer, as if Jonah had vanished into thin air. "You have a gift."

Her mouth dipped down in a frown, and she glanced at Jonah. "I thought that was a gift with horses, not half-grown—"

"Okay, Jonah," Jake said, cutting her off and turning to him. "I'll give you a try, but—"

"Yeah?" Jonah said, hoping he didn't sound too eager. "Thanks, Mr. Canfield. I won't disappoint you."

Jake puckered his mouth, but it turned into a smile. "I guess we'll see about that. We start early and work a long day."

"Okay."

"You have a place to stay?"

Jonah looked around and spied the barn. "The barn, there, would suit me fine, Mr. Canfield."

"It's Jake. Mr. Canfield is my father." A funny look crossed his face for a second, but it disappeared. "You can stay in the new bunkhouse. It isn't painted, but it should do."

"It sounds fine to me," Jonah said, glancing at the woman. "Anything with a roof is good, and a bed is even better." He couldn't believe his luck, and he would do whatever he had to do. Working on a real ranch had been something he'd always wanted to do but never thought he ever would. And now he would get to. He just hoped he didn't look too excited about it.

Jake put a hand on the woman's shoulder. "This is Erin Walker," he said, as she stood there, staring at him. "She's great with horses, and I'm sure she'll be able to answer any questions you might have about them or about cattle."

Erin Walker? E.W. were the initials on the letter he'd found. The letter that had started all of this. It couldn't be that easy, could it?

"I'll—" She cleared her throat and looked up at Jake, who removed his hand from her shoulder. "I'll be happy to help."

She didn't sound all that happy, but Jonah figured there were things going on that he didn't know about.

"I'll bring some sheets and blankets down later," Jake told them. "If you need some help, I'm sure Erin will lend a hand."

The smile he shot her was a killer, and Jonah had to dig his nails into his hands to keep from laughing. Yeah, something was going on, that was for sure. And whatever it was, he would find out who these people were and if they were who he'd come to find.

"Let's get you settled in, Jonah," she said, waving a hand for him to follow.

Jonah switched his duffel bag to his left hand and stuck out his right. "Thank you, again, Mr.—Jake."

"Bunkhouse is over there," Erin said, pointing beyond the barn.

After giving Jonah's hand a firm shake, Jake released it. "Better hurry, Jonah, or she'll leave you behind."

He did. With a smile of satisfaction. If his cell phone worked, he would leave his parents a message in a couple of days and tell them he had a job. He would keep in touch. When he felt like it, if only to keep them from looking for him. After all, they hadn't been honest with him. Why should he be honest with them?

Chapter Four

"I guess you know Jake pretty well."

Erin, making up one of the small beds in the bunkhouse, looked up at Jonah. "What makes you say that?"

The boy shrugged. "I don't know. Just the way you talked to each other."

Returning her attention to the sheets Kelly had brought to them, she tried to think of an answer. She couldn't tell the boy she didn't want to talk about it. That might make him ask more questions. But she could give him simple answers.

"We've known each other since we were

kids," she answered, "so, yes, we know each other well, as many neighbors do."

"You're friends."

She pressed her lips together and glanced at him. "We were, long ago."

"But you still are, right?"

"We haven't seen each other for a long time."

"But you're still friends. He knows a lot about you, too, I guess."

Her hands froze in the process of smoothing a wrinkle. *He doesn't know I got pregnant that night.* But of course she wouldn't say that. She couldn't. Not to anyone.

Straightening, she turned to look at him. "Why do you want to know all this?"

"Just curious," he said with a lift of one shoulder. "Isn't it a good idea to know a little bit about your boss?"

She accepted his reasoning. "I suppose it is." His questions were innocent, so she had no valid reason not to answer them. "He only spent summers here—he didn't live here year-round. His uncle owned this ranch, which is now his. When the time came for him to go off to college, he did. And then…" She shook her head. "To be honest, I don't know. You'd have to ask him."

"Oh."

Working quickly, she finished the bed, ready to get back to ranch work. The chore of getting Jonah settled in wouldn't have been her choice if she'd been asked. But if she would be working with him, she might as well try to make it as pleasant as possible for both of them.

"If you need anything else—"

"No, I'm good," he answered. "Thanks. I know how to make up a bed, but it's usually a mess."

"It's not a problem," she answered, and meant it. "Go ahead and put your things away, then come out to meet the rest of the wranglers. I'm sure Jake will introduce you. They're a nice bunch, when you get to know them, and I'm sure they'll answer any questions you might have."

He nodded when she started for the door. "Ms. Walker?"

She looked back at him and smiled. He had nice manners. "Call me Erin. I'm not much for the formal stuff."

He seemed to relax a little. Poor kid. He was probably scared. She could relate. A new place, new people and the feeling of not yet belonging. She'd felt the same when she'd first started on the rodeo circuit.

"Uh, Erin, I've been wondering..."

She readied herself for another question, hoping it wouldn't be personal. "About what?"

"The guy who told me where I could find this place? His name was Walker, too."

"Dylan or Luke?" she asked, knowing either of them would help out a stranger, especially a teenage boy.

"Dylan."

She smiled again. "He's my brother. His

ranch—the ranch where I grew up—borders this one on the east."

"Oh, yeah, well that makes sense. Is Luke your brother, too?"

"Yes, he's the youngest. I'm the oldest. Dylan hates that," she said, almost laughing.

"I don't have any brothers," Jonah said. "Or sisters, either."

"I envy you," she said, sighing, but then shook her head. "No, I don't mean that. My brothers are great. I don't know what I'd do without them." Her brothers might give her constant grief over some of her life choices, and they'd pestered her unmercifully, almost as much as Jake had, when they were kids. But she wouldn't have wanted to live her life without them.

Jonah sat on the new mattress of the bed next to his. "That's a nice thing to say about them."

She scrunched up her nose. "Don't tell them I said it. It would go to their heads."

Jonah laughed. "You must know a lot about horses. How long have you worked here?"

"A week, so you're not the only new one here."

"A week?"

She shook her head and laughed "Okay, not quite. This is the end of my first week."

"Do you have a husband? I mean, are you married?"

The question should have surprised her, but it wasn't the first time some young kid had asked her, and she grinned at him. "Why? Are you planning to ask me for a date?"

His face reddened, and he ducked his head. "No, just curious."

She didn't blame him for asking. "A natural thing, I guess," she admitted. "Most women my age would be. But I've been barrel racing in rodeos since I was younger than you." In fact, she'd only been a few years older when she'd set out on her own, after Luke had graduated from high school and hadn't returned, except for a few visits.

"You're a barrel racer?"

"I was." She didn't add that she was only on a break. Until she knew she could win again—and had enough money to return—she wouldn't go back.

"Wow," he said on a breath.

At the sound of voices outside, she walked to the door and opened it to hear Jake asking the men where she'd gone. "I'm here, getting Jonah settled in," she said, stepping outside and down the two steps. "Isn't that what you wanted me to do?"

"It's my fault, not hers."

Erin turned to see Jonah standing in the doorway of the bunkhouse. "He wanted to know a little about the operation here," she said, covering for the boy who'd covered for her. "I thought it would help to answer his questions."

Jake nodded. "Nobody's at fault. But Kelly could use a hand in the barn. Erin, why don't you take Jonah and introduce them to each other?"

"Sure," she answered as Jonah walked out to join them. "Barn's over there," she said, pointing to the barn where she and Jake had— "I'll catch up with you. I need to talk to the boss."

"Erin—" Jake said.

"Hang on a minute, Jake." When she was sure Jonah had walked out of earshot, she turned to Jake. "What's gotten into you, giving a kid—with no references and obviously no experience—a job?"

Jake shrugged, watching Jonah walk toward the barn. "Everybody deserves a chance. He seems eager to learn, the same as I was. I can use him, no matter how inexperienced he might be. You wanted to know what your job is? Now you know. You're his official trainer."

She blew out a breath to keep from giving him a piece of her mind she couldn't afford. She couldn't deny that she liked Jonah. He sure asked a lot of questions, though. She chalked that up to being young and, as he'd admitted, curious. "Okay," she told Jake. "You're the boss."

"Keep remembering that," he said with a smile she couldn't read.

"I have a suggestion, though."

His eyes narrowed as he looked down at her. "Do you now? About Jonah?"

She shook her head. "No. And you can take it or leave it, but I've been thinking. You've been taking all of us to the café every day, and it's a waste."

"A waste?"

"Time and money," she said, nodding. "Since this is a permanent operation, have you given any thought to hiring a cook?"

His gray eyes sparkled, and he seemed to be fighting a smile. "Are you applying for the job?"

She stared at him. "Me? Cook? Are you kidding? What makes you think I can cook?"

"Come on, Erin. You haven't been on a junk

food diet all those years in the rodeo. Not with that body."

Heat raced through her as he slowly looked her up and down. She needed to put a stop to her reactions to that. "That's not an appropriate—"

"And I doubt your brothers made do for themselves after your parents were gone."

"But I—"

"I know you put your plans on hold, until Luke graduated."

It wouldn't do any good to deny it. "That doesn't mean—"

"And I got a glimpse of that motor home of yours. No doubt it's tricked out with a nice kitchen."

Sighing, she'd had enough, even knowing he was teasing. "I don't want to apply for a job as a cook, here or anyplace else. I was only trying to be helpful, but if you—"

"I'm open to any suggestions you might have. Do you know someone who might be interested?"

She gave it some thought. "No, but I could ask around."

"I'd appreciate that," he said, his expression serious.

"You could put a flyer in the café, the way you did for the wrangler job. The grain elevator, too. Lots of people gather there, and someone might know about one."

"Good idea. I'll give it a try."

She relaxed and gave a quick nod. "I'll let you know if I hear about anyone you could hire."

"See?" he said, grinning at her. "That wasn't so hard, after all."

Maybe not, she thought. But there were things he didn't know that could change things in an instant if he learned about them. Not things. One thing. "I'll go give Jonah and Kelly a hand," she said as an excuse to get away. Getting along too well with Jake might not be the best thing to do.

"Take it easy on him, Erin," Jake said when she turned to walk away.

"Yes, boss," she said with a wave of her hand, and headed for the barn.

JAKE STOOD AT the counter inside the grain elevator office and signed his name to the bill of sale. But feed was the furthest thing from his mind. Instead, he kept thinking of Erin.

"We'll have that feed delivered first thing in the morning, Jake," the elevator manager told him.

The sound of the man's voice dragged Jake from his thoughts, and he looked up. "Thanks, Tom. Anytime before Saturday will be fine. I'll make a note to get it ordered earlier next time."

"Settin' up a new ranch can take some doing," Tom said, handing him a copy of the receipt. "What with new animals and new ranch hands… Say, I hear you hired the Walker girl."

Nodding, Jake answered, "She knows a lot about livestock."

"She was always a nice girl. Bit of a tomboy, but she took good care of those brothers of hers, after their parents died. Put her plans to join the rodeo on hold, until that youngest, Luke, graduated from high school."

"That's what the boys told me. She's a hard worker, too, not to mention she knows as much if not more than the rest of the hands."

"Heart of gold," Tom said.

Jake nodded. *Except when it comes to me.* He tucked the ticket into his shirt pocket, ready to leave, and remembered he'd brought Jonah with him.

"Have you seen—" He spied Jonah on the platform, watching a truck full of wheat unloading, and remembered he'd been just as curious when he was a kid.

"New wrangler?" Tom asked.

Jake nodded and smiled. "About as green as they come, but he's learning fast."

They watched as Jonah talked with one of the boys who worked at the elevator. Jake was pleased that he might be making friends in the area. Not only would he learn a lot from boys who'd been farming and ranching all their lives, but friends his own age would add some enjoyment to long days of ranching.

As if he heard them talking about him, Jonah walked inside. "I never knew there was so much work to a wheat harvest. You'd think there'd be an easier way," he said to the two men.

"Combines and tractors keep gettin' bigger," Tom said, "but the work doesn't change much. I remember back when none of them had cabs, much less air-conditioning."

"Before my time," Jake said. "David Walker used to tell stories about it, though." His uncle, on the other hand, didn't talk much. Dinnertime had always been strained, except when Uncle Carl was giving orders or complaining. Thinking of those dinners reminded him of Erin's suggestion.

"Are we done?" Jonah asked.

"In a minute," Jake said, turning to the manager. "Say, Tom, do you know if there's anybody around these parts that might be interested in cooking for a small group of ranch hands?"

"Man or woman?"

"Either. Just the noon dinner during the week."

Tom pulled off his gimme cap and scratched his head. "Not for sure, but Ada Sterling was looking for something to keep herself busy, now that the mister is gone."

"Sterling? I'm not familiar with the name."

"Ada ran the school cafeteria for thirty years or so. Ed, her husband, passed away a year or so ago, not long after she retired. The cooks at the school still use her recipes, and they're some of the best."

"I'll take that as a good reference and look into it. Thanks again, Tom." Motioning for Jonah to follow, he left the grain elevator.

Several people spoke to him on their way to the truck, and it took longer to get away than he'd thought it would. Climbing into his truck, he waited for Jonah, who'd stopped to talk to another boy. In the little time he'd been inside with Tom, the morning had warmed more than he'd expected. June was in full swing, and he wondered what the weather might do. It could be hot and dry, or wet and stormy, with an occasional tornado. No matter which, it promised to be a hot summer, and he hoped Erin kept an eye on the water tanks for the stock.

What was he thinking? Erin would take better care of his stock than he would. It was second nature to her. She'd been born into a ranching family and done chores long before he met her. He recalled her racing to catch up with him and her brothers, because she'd stayed behind to feed the numerous cats the Walkers had always kept around. She'd worked beside her dad and her brothers for as long as he could remember. Whether she liked him or not, he had no doubt she would be sure the animals were well taken care of.

Once Jonah got in the truck, he started the engine and headed for home. "I see you made a couple of friends," he said, as they turned out of the town and onto the county road.

"Yeah," Jonah answered. "But they're pretty busy right now. Did you know there's a hayrack ride Saturday evening? Some community thing."

"Hayrack ride? No, I hadn't heard." Not that he cared.

"Would it be okay if I go?"

Jake glanced at him. "As long as it isn't during the workday, you're on your own time. I'll give you a ride into town, if you need one."

"Thanks."

Determined to keep his focus on anything but Erin, he managed not to give much thought to her until he pulled into the driveway next to his house. From there, he could see her perched on the top fence railing of the big corral, the other hands standing around her, as if they were worshipping a goddess. He tried slamming the door of his truck loud enough to get their attention, but they didn't even bother to look his way, so he walked toward them. To make matters worse, they didn't notice when he stopped only a few feet from them.

"While the boss is away, the boys will play?" he asked.

Gary turned to look at him, then jabbed Bobby Ray with an elbow. "Just taking a water break," Gary explained, pointing to the ten-gallon watercooler sitting nearby. "Erin's been telling us about some of the rodeos she competed in."

Jake didn't care that they'd taken a break. They didn't punch a time clock at his place. And he was pleased they'd accepted her. He hadn't been sure they would. But the sight of them gathered around Erin made his teeth hurt. Frowning, he looked directly at her. "Do the horses have water?"

She started to answer, but Jonah, who had joined them, spoke first. "I made sure the tanks were full before we left for town."

With nothing else to ask or complain about,

Jake nodded. "I'm sure Erin's stories are fascinating, but let's save some of them for another time. We've got work to do."

He waited until they hurried back to their chores, and then he turned to walk away. He'd said all that needed saying and doubted he would have to mention it again. The men just hadn't gotten used to having her around. They would, but he wondered if he ever would.

"Hey, wait up!"

The voice was unmistakable, and he kept walking. Behind him, he heard boots hitting the ground at a trot.

"Thanks for the jog," Erin said, her voice dripping with sarcasm.

When she caught up with him, he didn't bother to look at her and kept walking. "Holding court, were you, Your Majesty?"

"Five minutes, Jake, no more. We can't take a five-minute break?"

He tried to think of a plausible answer but couldn't. Instead, he kept seeing her on that top rail, smiling down at everyone. And one of them had helped get her up there. He wanted to know who.

He turned his head to look at her. "Who put you up on that fence?" he asked, imagining someone putting his hands on her. He didn't like it one bit. And he wished it didn't matter.

Her eyes widened. "Is that it? Is that what has you growling at everybody?"

"No," he lied.

"Because if it is, you need to know that I climbed up there by myself."

"Do you realize that if you'd fallen, it would be on my head?"

Her braid whipped to her other shoulder when she tossed her head. "That's ridiculous."

He dug in a little deeper. "And knowing you, you'd probably sue me."

She came to a halt. "And just why would I do that?"

He stopped, too, and stared down at her. "Do you want the whole list or just the top five?"

When she ducked her head, he guessed at her next move. "Are you going to quit now?"

When she looked up, it was obvious he'd hit the mark. "Is that what you want me to do?"

"No." It was the last thing he wanted. "But I want you and all the others to be safe."

"It won't happen again."

Surprised that she didn't argue, he searched for something to say. "How's Jonah doing?"

Her eyes sparkled with her smile. "Good. He's going to saddle a horse on his own. Want to watch?"

"Sure," he answered, blasted from being the recipient of a big smile.

"Great! I'll go get him. We'll be in the south corral."

"I'll meet you there."

As she hurried away in search of their newest and youngest ranch hand, he reminded himself that her joy had been about Jonah, not him. He would be wise to keep that in mind.

Hoping the little exhibition would go well, he

walked on to the corral. It wasn't long before Erin arrived, leading one of the tamer horses, with Jonah behind her, lugging a saddle. Choking back a laugh, Jake settled back against the fence for the show.

Erin ground-tied the mare, then stepped back several feet. "She's all yours, Jonah. Show me your stuff."

Jake watched, impressed with Jonah's new skills, but he watched Erin, too. Standing with her hands in her back pockets, she gave encouragement, but no instructions to the boy. It reminded him of the time she'd taught five-year-old Luke how to swing out on a rope tied to a tree branch and drop into the pond. Luke had been skeptical and made up excuses, but Erin's patience and encouraging words had the little guy swinging, a little shaky, but exhilarated when he hit the water. She might be sassy and bossy at times, but she had the patience of a saint when needed.

"How was that?" Jonah asked, stepping back from the saddled horse.

Erin handed him the reins, then hugged him. "I told you that you could do it."

"I couldn't have done it without you teaching me," Jonah replied. "Can I ride now?"

Jake laughed, proud of both of them. Although Erin hadn't wanted him to hire Jonah, she'd obviously accepted it and had struck up a friendship with the boy. Jonah might not be familiar with horses and ranching, but he was proving he had not only the will, but the talent to learn.

"Good job, both of you," he called to them. "Take some time to enjoy the ride, Jonah." With a wave, he left the corral and started for the barn, only to be joined by Gary.

"Don't you think you were a little hard on us?"

Jake slid a look at him. "What makes you think so?"

Gary rubbed the side of his nose with his finger. "Well, for one thing, you aren't normally so grouchy."

"I'm not grouchy."

"Sure does look like it from here."

Looking at him full on, Jake said, "From here it doesn't. So what's your beef?"

Shaking his head, Gary glanced over his shoulder. "Normally, you would've joined us, at least for a few minutes. What is it about her that sticks in your craw?"

"Nothing."

Gary nailed him with a look that said he didn't believe him, and suddenly smiled. "So that's it."

"What?"

"She's the one."

Jake had a good mind to tell his friend to take a hike, but that would only add fuel to the fire. "What *one?* I don't know what you're talking about."

"Sure you do. Those ten years we've known each other gives me a little insight into what I do believe is the problem. I remember you once talking about some little bit of a girl that you'd left behind."

"I never said that," Jake argued, knowing full well he had. If he'd been able to see into the future, he never would have mentioned it. That's what an evening of kicking up your heels and drinking too much would get a person.

Putting a hand on his shoulder, Gary lowered his voice. "I won't tell anybody, because I know how you're feeling. It happens to all of us. So what are you going to do about it?"

Jake had asked himself the same thing, over and over, and he'd never come up with an answer he could live with. He'd hired her because he needed another wrangler, and she could do the job. He'd also sensed she needed it. But he knew he'd used that as an excuse. He'd done it to be closer to her, to see if he could win her back. So far, nothing had worked.

"I'm not going to do anything," he answered.

Gary gave his shoulder a pat. "A wise man never passes up a second chance."

Jake watched him walk away and thought about second chances. He'd been given one when his uncle left the ranch to him, and he intended to make it one of the best in the area. He had the know-how, and he had a crew that could help. And now he'd been given a second chance with Erin. He would be a fool to throw it away. He needed to do something.

ERIN TAPPED HER foot and looked around the approaching dark of late evening, wondering what might be keeping Jonah. All the other hay trailers had left the park, full of passengers. She'd left work early to help set up for the community event, but Jonah had told her he would be there. Had he forgotten and gone off with some of his new friends?

Ready to give up and tell Jimmy Tartelli, one of the volunteer drivers, she saw Jonah hurrying toward the rig. But she hadn't expected to see Jake with him or the girl who appeared to be around Jonah's age.

"Sorry we're late," Jake said, helping the other two onto the wagon.

"You're coming, too?" she asked.

Jake shrugged. "I stopped to talk to Dusty when I dropped Jonah off at the park. Jonah went to join a bunch of teenagers, and the next thing I knew, he asked me if I'd chaperone him and—"

"Her?" Erin asked, watching Jonah and the girl find a spot in the hay.

"Her name is Desiree," he said. "She's almost sixteen. Seems her parents wanted somebody to keep an eye on the two of them. Can't say I blame them."

"He probably met her in town when one of the boys picked him up the other night."

"That was one of the boys he met at the elevator," Jake said. "It's good that he's made some—"

"Is this everybody?" came a shout from the front of the wagon.

Erin looked around to make sure no one else might be coming their way. "I guess it is, Jimmy."

Jake helped her climb onto the wagon, and they sat down side by side. "Is this okay?" he asked.

She nodded. "You hadn't planned on coming?"

"No. And in case you're wondering, I didn't know you'd be here."

"I never thought—" She bit her lip, wishing she hadn't said it.

"So this is why you left early today?"

"I was roped into it," she answered with a sigh.

"You?" he asked as if it were the last thing that would ever happen.

"Yes, me. Glory asked if I'd help round up the wagons and drivers, and that led to…" She shrugged. "So here I am."

For several seconds, neither of them spoke. "It's a nice night for it," he said, looking up at the sky. "Couldn't ask for better weather."

Thinking he might believe she'd intentionally not told him about the hayrack ride, she leaned over to look at him. "I didn't know you might want to come along. In fact, I wouldn't be here if I hadn't had a hand in organizing it."

"No need to explain," he said without bothering to glance at her. "You don't answer to me."

"Or you to me," she added. But deep down she wished it could be different. She knew she should stay away from him, but working for him didn't make that easy. And the more time she spent with him, the harder it became for her. But there were things that needed to remain unsaid to him. Her secret had died with her parents. It needed to stay that way.

Jake cleared his throat. "How many trailers do we have?"

"We?"

"Okay, how many trailers do *you* have?"

"Six," Erin answered, "but we could have had more. Lots of people offered."

"Did you have any trouble finding drivers?" he asked her.

The movement of the trailer calmed her. "Believe it or not, we didn't. Once word went out, people were calling and volunteering."

"You've always been well liked in Desperation, so I'm not surprised."

She gave an unladylike snort. If the people in Desperation knew the truth about her… Unwed teen moms who went away and gave up their baby didn't sit too well with a lot of people. But they would never know. None of them.

The back wheel of the trailer hit a bump, knocking him closer. She didn't move away.

"Sorry about that, folks," Jimmy said from the front of the trailer. "I thought I could miss that. Did we lose anybody?"

On the other side of the trailer, Desiree giggled, then sneezed. "Gesundheit," Jonah exclaimed.

"We're still here, too," Jake said.

As they drove on, quiet blanketed the countryside outside of Desperation and the passengers on the trailer. Bits and pieces of whispers drifted from Jonah and Desiree's side, along with another sneeze.

"How do the drivers know where to go?" Jake asked.

As long as the conversation stayed neutral and on everyday things, Erin felt fine talking with him. "Believe it or not, I mapped a course for each one. We weren't supposed to be the last, but…"

"Plans don't always work out," Jake finished.

Erin thought of all the plans she'd had when she was Desiree's age and how some had worked out, but others hadn't. "It all comes down to choices," she whispered to herself.

"That's how we learn," he answered.

Turning to him, she saw him watching her, and her heart skipped a beat, as if it wanted her to hurry things along. "Sometimes the hard way."

"No kidding."

She yearned to know what had happened in his life, after he left his uncle's ranch. She knew he'd left the next day, but she hadn't seen or heard from him all these years. And even though she'd tried to forget him, she hadn't. She'd only locked the memories away. Until now.

"Why did you quit school?" she asked.

He sat close enough to her that she felt his shrug. "Because I got bored and wanted to do something else."

"What did you want to do?"

"Work on a ranch. Learn more about ranching. Maybe have my own someday."

And yet he still didn't return to Desperation. The thought made her heart hurt. "And now you do. I'm thinking those college business classes probably helped."

"Maybe a little," he admitted. "Those summers here were a big part of it. Uncle Carl taught me a lot, even though he wasn't crazy about doing it. And I learned from your dad and your brothers. You, too."

She shook her head, remembering her parents and how they'd struggled. "Pop wasn't the best at business," she said, "but Luke and Dylan learned a lot from that, I guess. Look how successful they are now."

"They are, and they're a gold mine of information." He paused for a moment. "But you helped. You gave up two years of rodeo for them."

She hated when people pointed that out. "I didn't really have a choice, did I?"

"Sure you did, and you took on a responsibility you never expected to have."

Thinking back to those two years, she silently agreed. "They couldn't go it alone. I'm the oldest. Dylan was so devastated by the accident that I worried about him. If I hadn't stayed…"

"But you did."

"Do you know that it wasn't until about a year ago, when Glory returned, that he finally pulled himself together and out of the past? And now he's living in the here and now, and looking forward to the future. There's no way I can ever thank her for that." Laughing softly at her own role in that little scheme, she added, "But then if it hadn't been for me sticking my nose into his business, they might never have gotten together."

"So you're a matchmaker now?"

Before she could answer, she heard noises and looked behind her to see Jonah crawling across the hay toward her.

"I guess Desiree is allergic to the hay," he said, obviously disappointed. "Would it be okay if we walk back to her place?" He turned to Jake. "I don't think her mom would mind, considering, and I promise to be a gentleman."

Erin watched Jake's face in the moonlight. His mouth tightened, and she wondered if he might be thinking the same thing she was. *Even a gentleman could lose control with the right woman.*

"Erin?" Jake asked.

"It's all right with me," she answered, surprising herself. "Do you know the way?" she asked Jonah.

"Two miles over that way." He pointed to the east.

"Jimmy?" Jake called out. "Do you know where Desiree lives?"

"Sure do," Jimmy answered. "Just down the road apiece. They'll be safe. My place is a quarter of a mile from her folks'."

"All right," Jake told Jonah. "But if you have any trouble, just yell."

"The only trouble will be when her mom finds out she didn't take her allergy medicine. All that sneezing and itching." He shook his head.

Concerned, Erin asked, "Itching? Good grief, you need to get her home as soon as possible."

"That's what I plan to do."

"I'll swing by and pick you up when this is over," Jake said.

Jimmy slowed the trailer and waited for Jonah and Desiree to jump off. With a promise from Jonah to get her home safely and quickly, the two were on their way.

Feeling suddenly very tired, Erin fell back in the straw. "What a day," she said with a sigh.

"And what a night," Jake whispered. Moving to lie beside her, he propped his head on his hand. "Now what?"

"Sleep," she answered, followed by a yawn.

"You can't go to sleep," he told her.

Turning her head to look at him, she asked, "Why not?"

His smile was slow and easy as he leaned closer. "Because if you do, you'll miss this."

Closing her eyes, she held her breath and then felt his soft, warm breath on her face a second before his lips were on hers. She knew she shouldn't, but she enjoyed it. She always had and probably always would. That could only mean trouble.

Chapter Five

The sun had already set when Jake pulled into his driveway, a week after the hayrack ride. Exhausted from the over twelve-hour drive from Flagstaff, Arizona, his bed and a late morning were the only things on his mind. How had Erin done it for so many years on the circuit?

Before he made it into the house with his traveling bag and a backside that ached from riding in his truck for half a day, Jonah appeared.

"How did you all do this week while I was gone?" Jake asked the boy, who followed him to the porch.

"As a whole, pretty good."

"No problems?"

"None with the ranch that I know of, but..."

With his hand on the doorknob, Jake stopped and turned his head to look at him. "But what?"

Jonah took a step back. "You look kind of tired. I'll tell you in the morning."

Frustrated and bone weary after spending a week away from home, Jake shook his head and opened the door. "No, tell me now, or I won't get any sleep, wondering what it is."

"Why don't I put your pickup in the garage?"

"*Now,* Jonah. No more excuses." The boy silently followed him into the kitchen, where Jake pointed to the refrigerator. "There's a can of frozen orange juice in the freezer. Get it out, and I'll fix a pitcher of it for us. Coffee will just mess me up."

Nodding, Jonah went to the freezer without a word.

Wishing for hours and hours of sleep, Jake pulled two tall glasses from the cabinet. "And put some ice in these."

Jonah took them from him, while he found a

pitcher and started running cold water from the faucet. That was what he needed to stay awake long enough to hear what Jonah had to tell him.

After taking the frozen juice and ice-filled glasses from Jonah, he finished the task and pointed to the stools on the other side of the breakfast bar. "Have a seat."

Jonah glanced in the direction of the door. "Don't you want to sit down?"

Tired but still keyed up after the long drive, Jake took a deep breath and blew it out. "I've been sitting in a pickup for over twelve hours, hoping to make good time. The scenery on the drive was beautiful, but at this point, all I want to do is stand. Besides, I'd probably fall asleep the second my butt hit a chair."

"That might be a good thing," Jonah muttered.

Jake ignored him. "Now, what kind of non-ranch-related problem are we talking about?"

Jonah stared into his glass of orange juice. "I'll give you one guess."

Finishing off a gulp of juice with a sigh, Jake set his glass down. "I'm guessing this has something to do with a young lady who's employed here?"

Nodding, Jonah still didn't look up.

"Why am I not surprised?" Jake asked no one before focusing on Jonah. "What is it this time?"

"You didn't tell her you'd be gone."

"Sure I did. I told all of you that I'd be going to the sale in Wichita Falls and— Has that bull been delivered yet?"

"Thursday."

"Good, good. I paid a pretty penny for him, let me tell you."

"Erin gave him her seal of approval."

Jake grunted. That sounded just like her. And she probably thought he would be pleased that she'd given it. Without meaning to, he smiled. "You think that's a problem?"

"No," Jonah said, raising his eyes to Jake.

"The problem is that you didn't tell her you were leaving."

"I did, too."

Jonah's gaze didn't waver. "She left early that day before the hayrack ride, when you told the rest of us. I guess we never thought to mention it to her. I figured you'd told her yourself."

"Damn." He really had screwed up.

"The sale supposedly closed on Tuesday, so when you weren't back by Wednesday evening, she asked if I knew why you were late." Jonah rubbed his forehead with his thumb. "I told her you were going to Arizona to see a friend and you'd be back yesterday or today. That's what you told us."

Jake nodded. He should have made sure she knew, but it had been crazy that week before the hayrack ride. He'd had arrangements to make for a place to stay in Wichita Falls and phone calls to make to line up transportation for anything he bought there. At the last minute, he'd decided to drive to Flagstaff to see an old friend.

And then along came the hayrack ride, and he'd been so wrapped up in her after that kiss and the ones that followed, that he forgot to mention the trip. All he could think about as he drove those long hours had been Erin and how one small step had become a big one. The one he would now admit that he'd been hoping for since the day he'd heard his uncle had died and he would be going back to Desperation, although he hadn't expected to see her.

"I'll talk to her when she gets here on Monday," he told Jonah.

"You'll be lucky if she listens," Jonah replied, and took a drink of the orange juice. "She's one mad woman right now. I can't say that I blame her."

Jake took the words to heart and wondered just how bad he'd blown it. "I suppose she has the right to be," he conceded.

"You really want to hook up with her, don't you?"

Stunned by the question, all Jake could do was look at the boy. Just how much should he admit? "Since I was fifteen."

Jonah's mouth dropped open. "That long?"

Jake lifted a shoulder. "We've known each other since we were kids. Every summer, since I was eight and she was six, I stayed with my uncle, until I went off to college."

"And you still couldn't hook up with her?"

Jake's mind flashed back to those last two or three summers. "We did. Sort of."

Sort of? That put it a bit mildly. That last summer, they'd endured daily teasing from her brothers. And then in the fall, at Thanksgiving time, he'd returned, still in love with her but knowing it wouldn't work out for them. And he hadn't known how to tell her. When he did—

He shook the memory from his head. "It's almost like starting over again," he said, not realizing he said it aloud.

"You know, Jake, it wouldn't be as hard as you think to pick up where you left off."

Jake's focus zeroed in on Jonah. "Do you know something I don't?"

Sighing, Jonah shook his head. "But I know she's into you. Everybody can see that."

Jake's interest shot up. "Yeah?"

Jonah nodded with a smile. "The other guys and I were talking about it the other day." Jake groaned, but Jonah continued. "I saw it that first day," he added with a smug smile. "To tell the truth, if I were you, I'd feel the same way. She's something else."

Jake couldn't deny it. "Yeah, she is, but she's a little old for you," he said with a chuckle. "But that doesn't solve the problem." Moving away from the counter, he tried to clear his tired mind. He could wait until Monday, but if she was as mad as Jonah said, he might want to talk to her sooner.

"You go on to bed," he told Jonah, "and I'll

sleep on it. I'll check on her tomorrow and see if I can smooth things over."

Lord, he hoped he could.

The next morning, he and Jonah finished the few chores that needed to be done in record time, and he set off for the Walker ranch.

As soon as he arrived, he noticed her RV, parked near the line of trees that separated the two properties. As he started to walk around it, he heard a female voice in the distance, coming from the vicinity of the barn. The whinny of a horse followed, answered by a shout of "No! This way." Smiling, he stayed back, watching from the side of a newer outbuilding next to the barn. From there, he had a prime spot to watch her and hear what she said to her horse. And she had plenty to say.

"Look, Duff, it's easy," she said from her saddle. Turning the horse back to the start of the barrels that were set up in the corral, she kept talking. "It's right, left, then left again to the homestretch. What's so hard about that?"

He heard the frustration in her voice and wished he could help, but although he'd watched barrel racing, he didn't know enough to give her any tips—if she would even listen to him, and he doubted she would.

Seated in the saddle like the pro she was, she backed MacDuff to what must have been the starting line. She leaned forward, giving him a double kick, and off they went, dust swirling around the ground beneath them.

The first barrel seemed to go well, as she and MacDuff rounded it to head for barrel two. Jake watched as the horse hesitated but kept going. At the third barrel, the horse started to go right. Erin tried to urge him left, but the horse wouldn't stand for it. She allowed him to go his way, and then pulled up as soon as the turn had been made.

"Stupid horse!" she shouted, swinging her leg over the saddle and sliding to the ground. "Don't you know your right from your left?"

Jake had never heard her talk to an animal

that way. Erin had always kept her emotions in check during training or practice.

Out of the corner of his eye, he saw Dylan walking across the ranch yard, shaking his head. “Patience, Erin,” he said when he came close enough to be heard. “Isn’t that what you always told us?”

Even from a distance, Jake could see the killer look she gave her brother. “I’m all out of patience with this mule-headed animal. He’s worthless.”

Dylan stopped at the fence and propped his folded arms on the top rail. “Stop expecting him to be like Firewind.”

Walking toward her brother, the horse left behind, she pulled off her hat and slammed it against her thigh. “I don’t. But if I did, he wouldn’t measure up. He’s not even close to what Firewind was, and he never will be.”

“It’s all in your head,” Dylan said. “Firewind was just as green as MacDuff is when you got him. Be patient.”

"I don't have time."

Detecting a hoarseness in her voice, Jake felt a pain in his chest. That particular sound was a sure sign tears were about to spill. And then it hit him that she seemed to have some kind of deadline. Did she plan to go back to the circuit?

"Hey, Jake!" Dylan shouted, waving.

Wishing he hadn't been seen until he could make sense of what he'd heard, Jake halfheartedly lifted a hand in greeting. The deep frown on Erin's face, as she looked in his direction and slammed her hat back on her head, told him all he needed to know. She didn't like that he'd been watching her. Add that to her anger that he hadn't told her about the longer trip, and he was in over his head.

Moving from his spot, he soon joined them but turned his attention to Dylan. "I came by to see you about some ranching business, but when I saw Erin, I stayed back. No sense spooking her or MacDuff." It sounded legitimate to him, but the soft snort from Erin said she didn't believe it.

"Come on up to the house," Dylan said, backing away from the fence. "You know how Erin doesn't like an audience while she's practicing."

"Practicing?" Erin asked, the word dripping with sarcasm. "Trying to teach a dumb animal is more like it."

Jake looked her in the eye. "Patience isn't one of your virtues today, is it?"

Eyes narrowing, her chest rose with a deep breath, but instead of answering, she spun on her heel and walked away, her back ramrod straight.

"Not exactly the best thing to say to her right now," Dylan said, keeping his voice low.

"You know as well as I do that sometimes she needs to get mad to get her moving in the right direction and do what needs doing."

Dylan turned to look at him. "Yeah, but there's something different this time."

That got his attention. “What kind of something?”

“I’m not sure,” Dylan said, shaking his head. “I saw her come home early from your place on Friday, after the hayrack ride and— Say, you didn’t miss that, did you?”

“No, I didn’t miss it. Nice night,” Jake answered. Not that he would give any details, or even the fact that he’d shared the ride with Erin. “But there’s been a little misunderstanding where your sister is concerned. You remember how those were.”

Chuckling, Dylan slapped his back. “How could I forget them? You two were always at each other about something or other. I’d kind of hoped that had ended when she took the job at your ranch.”

“It’s gotten better,” Jake admitted. “I get the feeling that she likes the job. I give her as much free rein as I can, and she’s doing a great job. But once in a while… Let’s just say we disagree.”

"That's a good way to put it."

Relieved that he'd gotten away without revealing anything, they spent the next twenty minutes talking about ranching. When they were done, with a promise from Dylan to return the visit in the near future and permission to swim in the pond at any time, Jake started for home. Seeing that Erin had returned to the training, he was tempted to avoid the corral. But he owed her an apology for leaving her out of the loop about the trip. Whether she accepted it or not, he still needed to explain.

And he still felt a little shaken about her comment that she didn't have time. Her dark mood could mean many things, and he hoped it wasn't about a plan to return to barrel racing. He wanted her to stay. He wanted to make up for what had happened between them, but he wondered if it would ever be possible.

"Is it going any better?" he asked.

"Not much," she answered, on her horse again.

"Do you have a minute?"

"That's about all I have," she said, but didn't move.

He had no choice but to jump right in and say what needed to be said. "I didn't realize you weren't aware that I planned to go to Flagstaff. I didn't decide until Friday afternoon, after you'd left to help out with the hayrack ride and—"

"You had plenty of time to tell me that night."

He couldn't deny it. "I guess I was busy with something more important," he said. He saw her face flush, and he hid his smile. "I'm sorry I forgot to tell you."

"All right."

"Does that mean I'm forgiven?"

"Yes, I guess it does."

"I won't forget again."

With a nod and a brief smile, she gave MacDuff a nudge, and they rode away. At least, he thought, she understood. And he sure as hell wouldn't repeat the mistake.

ERIN STEPPED OUT of her motor home to find Sollie waiting by her steps. “Did Jake send you to get me?” she asked, scratching the spot between the dog’s ears. “He doesn’t need to, you know. I don’t have a choice. It’s either work and earn the money I need, or be at my brothers’ mercy. I’d rather work, even if it means seeing your master every day.”

Sollie’s answer was the rapid shake of his tail, complete with lolling tongue. Laughing, Erin snapped her fingers at him, and they started on their way to the ranch. “Monday and the start of my fourth week. He’s a pretty good boss. Imagine that.”

When they reached the ranch, Sollie ran off and she saw Jonah coming out of the bunkhouse.

“Hey, Erin,” he greeted her. “You’re here early.”

“Trying to impress the boss,” she joked. “Are you up for some real work today?”

He looked at her as if he hadn't heard right. "Yeah."

Nodding, she smiled at him. "Jake mentioned that there are some cattle in the west pasture that need to be put with the rest of the herd, and he thought you might like to help me bring them up."

"When do we start?"

"As soon as he gives us the okay, and hopefully before it gets too hot." Shading her eyes, she looked toward the house and saw Jake coming down the back steps, a cup in his hand. "Here he comes. Now, don't act too excited. Sometimes he can be a real killjoy."

"Good morning, you two," Jake hailed them, raising his cup high. "There's coffee and some of Ada Sterling's cinnamon rolls on the porch, if you want some."

As soon as Erin realized what he'd said, she sprinted over to him and grabbed his arm, causing him to slosh coffee over the side of his cup. "I'm sorry," she said, but forgot about it immediately. "Ada's cinnamon rolls? Jake, they're heavenly!"

"They sure are," he said with a wide grin.

"That's who you need to hire to cook," she blurted.

"Is that so?"

Excited at the thought of having Ada cook for them, she could hardly stand still, then noticed she hadn't let go of Jake's arm. Releasing him, she stepped back. "Yes, it is. You can't go wrong with Ada. She's one of the best in the county. Probably the whole state."

Jake glanced down, then up again, wearing a frown. "Maybe you should be the one to talk to her."

"I suppose I could, but—" She saw a flash of something in his eyes and couldn't contain her excitement. "She's here, isn't she?"

His frown disappeared and he nodded, obviously trying to hide a smile. "Go on inside and see her," he said. "She's been asking for you."

Without thinking, she jumped up and threw

her arms around his neck. "Oh, thank you, Jake."

"Um, Erin?" he whispered.

Realizing that the other hands were arriving, she let go and hurried to the house. "I won't be long," she called back to him. "I only want to say hello."

She hadn't seen Ada since she'd left for the rodeo, but she'd never forgotten her. Ada had helped her through the death of her parents, giving her advice about everything from cooking to how to get through the sorrow of losing them. It had been Ada who had finally told her to hit the road and bring back a silver buckle.

Opening the door to what she hoped was the kitchen, Erin called out to her. "Ada? It's Erin Walker. Are you too busy for an old friend?"

From around the corner, Ada appeared, all smiles and a big white apron. "There's my girl," she cried, and hurried to wrap her arms around Erin. "Lawsy, girl, I haven't seen you for forever."

Tears pooled in Erin's eyes. "It's been so long," she said around the huge lump in her throat. Ada's soothing pats calmed her quickly, and she looked up into the dark face and eyes she remembered from her childhood. "I can't believe you're here."

"Mr. Canfield called me up last night," Ada said, stepping back to rub her hands up and down Erin's arms, calming her. "I remembered that you and he were friends from way back and asked about you. When he told me you were home and workin' for him, I couldn't refuse his offer."

"You don't know how happy I am that you're here," Erin said, drying her tears with her hands.

"I guess it hasn't been easy for you workin' for the man who broke your heart."

Erin pressed her lips together. Ada had been the first person she'd told about the baby and had helped her and her parents to make the right decision. "At first," she admitted. "But—"

Ada nodded. "The years can make it easier. I'm glad the two of you are on good terms."

Good? Erin didn't know for sure if she'd call it *good.* Strange, yes. Sometimes even wonderful. "We get along," she answered. "But, Ada, he doesn't know."

Eyes wide, Ada looked at her. "About— You've got to tell him, honey."

"Maybe," Erin answered.

"Soon," Ada said, watching her.

"I know," she said, "and I will." She took a big breath and smiled. "But right now, I've got a young cowboy that needs some lessons in rounding up cattle."

"You go on, then, Miz Erin. I'll be around whenever you have a spare minute or two."

"I'll give you more than a minute or two," Erin promised.

She left the house, feeling both better and afraid. But with Ada by her side, she could weather just about anything.

"Are you planning to bring up the cattle from

the west pasture?" Jake asked, standing with Jonah.

"Can Jonah lend me a hand?" she asked, knowing Jake had already okayed it. She wanted Jonah to hear it for himself.

Jake put his hand on Jonah's shoulder. "I think that's a great idea. Nothing like on-the-job training, right, Jonah?"

"Sure. I'm ready when Erin is. And thanks for the opportunity."

"Go ahead and saddle up the horse you had the other day." Jake patted his shoulder. "Let me know how it goes."

Fifteen minutes later, Erin turned to Jonah as they entered the pasture. "You're handling that horse well."

Riding next to her, Jonah gave her a sheepish grin. "I wasn't supposed to say anything, but Jake let me practice yesterday."

Surprised and pleased, she grinned and didn't bother to hide it. "Did he, now?"

Jonah nodded. "Don't tell him I told you, though."

"I won't breathe a word of it," she answered, laughing. "Let's get this done."

"I guess you've always ridden," he said.

She smiled, thinking of happier times from the past. "My dad always said I was born on a horse."

"Jake said the same thing."

Uncomfortable that Jake had been talking about her, she wondered what Jake had told him. Instead of commenting, she changed the subject. "See those two heifers over there?" she asked, pointing farther out in the pasture. When he nodded, she asked, "Think you can get them here with the others?"

His eyes narrowed as he looked to where she pointed. "On my own?"

"You won't know if you don't try, right?" She waited for an answer, while he watched the cattle and fidgeted with the reins. "I'll be here to help, if you need it," she added. When he turned to look at her, she saw the indecision in his eyes. Expressive eyes. *Like Jake's.* She'd always known what Jake was feeling, even when they were kids.

He sat perfectly still, and then his shoulders rose and fell with a breath, and he urged his horse forward, his back straight and tall. She watched, ready to move if needed. Once or twice, when the heifers were giving him a run for his money, she nearly gave the gelding a soft nudge. But each time, Jonah managed to regain control and was soon heading the cattle toward her, smiling.

"You were right," he said when he reached her. "How did you—"

"Sometimes you just have to believe in yourself and then prove it."

Smiling, he shook his head. "You really *are* something special."

Feeling her face heat with embarrassment, she turned away. "Let's get them to the corral. You stay with those two, and I'll handle these."

"They gave me some trouble there, for a minute," he said, laughing. "But I got them rounded up, and it was like they knew I wasn't kidding around, that I knew what I was doing."

"That's what it takes," she told him, pleased that he'd been so successful on his first roundup. It didn't matter that he'd only dealt with two. He'd only needed to realize he could do it. Jake had known that.

As they rode on to the ranch, he asked, "What are your brothers like?"

She thought about it for a minute. "Dylan is quiet. Or was, especially after our parents died, but he's coming around. Luke is more happy-go-lucky. He has a son, Brayden, who's three, and a real cutie."

"They sound nice," Jonah said. "I'd like to meet them someday."

"I'm sure they'd like to meet you, too," Erin answered. "In fact, Dylan is having a barbecue Saturday night. I'll wrangle an invitation for you. Jake, too."

At the ranch, Jake opened the corral gate so they could herd the cattle inside. When Erin rode by him, she smiled and nodded to let him know all had gone well.

"Good job, Jonah," Jake called to him, shutting the gate behind them. "How'd it go?"

Erin remained silent and let Jonah answer.

"Good. Really good. But Erin deserves the credit. I would've backed out if she hadn't convinced me I could do it."

Jake's quick glance at her was too brief for her to decipher. "She doesn't let anybody back out."

Except for you, she thought. That one time. But she hadn't had much choice. He'd told her they both needed to go their own way, him back to college and her to the rodeo circuit.

"Go on up and get some water," Jake told him. "Or some orange juice. I put some out for you."

"You can leave your horse out here," she added. When Jonah had hurried away, she turned to Jake. "You knew it, didn't you?"

"Knew what?"

"That he needed to do it on his own to get the confidence he needed."

He nailed her to the spot with his gaze. "Not on his own, exactly. You were there."

"But how did you know?"

His soft smile did its usual trick of making her heart somersault, before he answered. "You don't remember?"

She shook her head. She'd forgotten as much as she could. It had been easier that way.

"You did the same thing to me that first time you and your brothers let me ride along with you."

At the mention of that day, the scene played itself out in her mind. He'd still been green with the horses. His uncle had rarely allowed him to take one out to ride. But because he was going with the Walker kids, he'd gotten the okay, as long as he did as he was told.

They'd been rounding up cattle, as she and Jonah had earlier. She'd been the one, not her brothers, who had told Jake to just go do it. And he had. When he'd brought the cattle up to the gate, where she and her brothers were waiting for him, her brothers applauded and whistled…scaring off the cattle and sending Jake to round them up again. The second time had been better.

"Now that you mention it, I do remember," she admitted.

"Yeah, me too. Clearly," he said, chuckling in that sexy way he had. "I didn't know whether to hug you or smack you. You were always such a know-it-all."

"So you always said," she replied.

"Haven't you learned yet that I'm always right?"

"Sure," she answered, flashing him a smile as she walked past him. "Except when you aren't." Behind her, she heard him laughing.

BY THE END of the week, the temperature hit new highs. Summer had come on full force, and everyone began wishing for a good, old-fashioned downpour. Instead, they were the ones who were dripping—and not because of rain.

Jake sent everyone home early and watched Erin until she disappeared from sight, as he always did. Sighing, he started for his house, eager for a cold shower—for more than one reason. He reached the back porch, only to discover Jonah sitting on the steps, fanning himself with the cowboy hat Jake had brought him from Arizona.

"You don't look so good," he told the boy.

"Headache," Jonah answered, rubbing the space between his eyes with his fist.

Jake took pity on him. "Come on inside," he said, motioning for Jonah to follow him. "But I get the shower first."

"I always forget that it's hotter the farther south you go," Jonah grumbled. "It's going to take more than a shower."

Jake looked over his shoulder as he reached

for the door. "There's always the big water tank."

"With this sun today?" Jonah grimaced. "A cool, dark place is what I need. I'll go back to the bunkhouse, if that's all right," he said, slowly getting to his feet.

"Why don't you go on into the house, take some aspirin or something and get cool? You can have the place to yourself. Leave the lights off or whatever you need."

"I guess I can. What are you going to do?"

As soon as Jonah asked, Jake knew. "Take a swim in the pond, also known as Lake Walker." He turned to walk back down the steps.

"What about trunks?" When Jake looked at him, he hurried to explain. "You know, swim trunks?"

"Don't need 'em. I'll swim in my Skivvies." He shot the boy a grin. "Or not. You go get cool and get some rest. Erin's brother invited us to a barbecue tomorrow night, and you don't want to miss it."

After making sure Jonah went into the house, Jake set out for the pond. By the time he reached the trees, he felt hotter than he'd been before he'd started. But the lure of the water, sparkling in the sun peeking through the leaves of the surrounding trees, promised blessed relief.

Eager to get into the pond, he quickly shed his hat, boots and clothes, then waded into the water. It cooled him the minute he scooped up a handful of it. Wading a little deeper, he leaned back, ready to float on the surface.

"Who the hell is in my pond?"

Erin? Jake nearly fell backward, but righted himself, in spite of one foot slipping on the muddy bottom. *Now what?*

"Jake Canfield, is that you?"

He heard her mutter something else and looked back over his shoulder, debating if he could make it to the bank before she came around the bend in the shore. He was still considering his options when he saw Erin swimming out to the deepest part of the pond.

"Can't I even get some quiet, personal time, without you barging in on me?" she asked, obviously treading water.

With only the top of her shoulders visible, he couldn't tell if she was as naked as he was, and he almost hoped she was. "I didn't know," he answered, making sure the water kept the lower half of him covered.

"Yeah, sure," came her sarcastic comeback. But she swam closer. "And I suppose you have permission?"

"As a matter of fact, I do. Dylan's permission."

He watched her moving in the water, getting closer and closer, until he could tell when her feet hit the bottom and she started walking. "You're welcome to check on that."

A smile he recognized from long ago lifted the corners of her mouth, but she hesitated.

"Maybe you should head back home. After all, I was here first."

Each step she took in his direction, the water level dipped lower. He held his breath, waiting. *Is she or isn't she?* But holding his breath didn't stop anything else that had started to rise to the unusual occasion, and he swallowed hard, just as the waterline moved down a little more.

A bikini. She had on a bikini. No straps, and no telling how skimpy the bottom might be, considering the small size of that top. He couldn't seem to move away from her.

"Stay right there," he said, holding up a dripping hand.

"Why?" she asked, still smiling as she moved closer.

His body throbbed as he wondered how far this might go. He watched a drop of water fall from the hair around her face and trickle down her skin, before it disappeared under the wisp of a top. She was so close, he could have touched her.

"I suppose I should tell you that I'm not wearing—"

"How dare you come here and think you can skinny-dip with me."

"I didn't—"

"Move an inch, and I'll scream so loud Dylan will hear me and come running with his shotgun."

"Is that so?" He reached out and traced her collarbone with his finger, smiling at the goose bumps it produced. "And which one of us do you think he'll shoot?"

"Jake…" she whispered, shivering.

"Cold?" He slipped his arm around her waist and pulled her closer. "How's that?"

"Better, but…"

He pulled her even closer and felt the warmth of her body. "Much better."

Lowering his head, he kissed her, and she pressed against him. When he thought he might explode any minute, she pulled away. "What?" he asked, thinking he might have scared her.

"Who did you say you went to see in Arizona?"

"Bowie," he answered.

"That name sounds familiar."

"It should," he said, smiling at her. "You probably know him."

Her face scrunched as she thought about it. "Bowie...Bowie..." Her eyes suddenly grew wider. "Bowie McClure? Oh, my— He's a world champion calf roper! And he's a friend of yours?"

"A good friend," Jake answered. "For several years, in fact. I've been trying to talk him into moving here. I have some acreage—"

"To Desperation?" she asked. "Why would he want to come here?"

He turned the tables on her. "Why did *you* come back?"

Looking away, she shrugged. "Because it's home. It always has been."

"I know that feeling." He tipped his head back and looked at the sky. "Maybe we should find some shade."

"No, I'm fine. But Bowie McClure in Desperation?"

He couldn't believe her fascination with someone he knew well. "He wants to move his futurity facility from Flagstaff, and I have some acreage on the other side of town, so I suggested—strongly—that he come take a look."

"He hasn't competed lately, has he?"

Jake shook his head. "No, he lost his wife a few years ago, and he left rodeo."

She ducked her head. "I'm so sorry to hear that. He has so much talent, and he's a very nice man. I met him a couple of times, and he's a real gentleman. Not that you aren't," she quickly added. "He'd fit really well in Desperation. Did you talk him into it?"

"I think I did. He's going to give me a call in a couple of weeks. There's a half-finished house on the property, and he'll need to have the buildings for the futurity built. It wouldn't take all that long, but he has a lot to think about.

Should I tell him you're eager for him to move here?"

She laughed. "I doubt he remembers me."

He hated to tell her, but he had to. "Actually, he does."

"Really?"

At that moment, she looked more vulnerable than he'd ever seen her. Younger. And thrilled that some guy who had roped calves for a living and won a couple of big, shiny buckles would remember her. "You're hard to forget, Erin."

The thrill on her face disappeared, replaced by something soft and warm, and she looked at him. Really looked at him. "So are you, Jake."

She wrapped her arms around his neck, and he felt something go through him, something he didn't recognize. Almost peaceful, but more powerful. All he could think of was how much he wanted to make her his, body and soul.

Chapter Six

Hayley, Luke's bride-to-be, held out a bowl of potato salad to Erin. "Would you mind taking this out and putting it on the table? Luke needs more barbecue sauce for the ribs, and bottled won't do, so I need to get busy with that."

"Bottled barbecue sauce?" Erin asked, holding the back of her hand to her forehead in fake shock. "Not in the Walker house." She took the big bowl from Hayley with a sigh. "Better get used to it. We have our traditions and nothing will change them."

Hayley wrinkled her nose. "I don't have a problem with traditions, but if he'd told me

I would need to triple your mom's recipe, I would have."

Cradling the bowl in one arm, Erin gave Hayley a quick hug. "He's a man. They forget. I'm surprised he trusts you with the recipe. He's never shared it with me." She produced a pout that made Hayley giggle.

"Don't you worry about that," Hayley assured her. "I'll share with you."

Erin peeked into the pan of sauce and sniffed. "You know what? I think this is *my* recipe, that thief."

Hayley laughed and stopped stirring. "Yours? It figures."

Leaning closer, Erin whispered, "Be thankful I introduced you to Luke, not Dylan. If he had the recipe, we'd have to pry it from his cold, dead hands."

"I'll bet Glory doesn't have to," Hayley said with a wink.

"Probably not," Erin admitted. "She has him wrapped around her little finger."

"Mommy! Mommy!"

Erin looked toward the door to see her three-year-old nephew rush into the kitchen and throw his arms around Hayley's knees. Her heart filled with love for the little guy, yet ached at the same time. She would never know what her son had been like at the same age. He would be almost seventeen now, and the thought made her sad. She'd missed so much, but she knew she had made the right choice. For herself and especially for him. Maybe someday—

She nearly dropped the bowl of potato salad when Brayden latched himself to her legs. "Hey, Brayden," she said, balancing the bowl as she gave him a hug. "Are you having fun?"

"Lots of fun!" Brayden yelled. "Daddy says I'm a big help."

"I'm sure you are," she told him. She looked up at Hayley, who smiled at them as she watched. "It's so good to see him so happy. If it hadn't been for you, stepping in as his nanny, and now getting ready to be the mommy he should have had…"

Hayley put her arm around her. "It wouldn't have happened if you hadn't sent me for the job interview. You've made all of us very happy."

Erin hated showing emotions, although lately it kept happening more and more often, and she blinked back the tears that threatened. Brayden immediately set up a hue and cry for the cookies that filled a plate on the counter, and she managed to escape the room without notice. On the screened-in porch, she pulled herself together, knowing deep down that she'd been blessed with the life she'd chosen. Maybe she'd left the rodeo earlier than planned, but she would go back again, soon, and come out a winner. Children weren't in her future, except for Brayden and the nieces and nephews that would come later.

"There you are," Glory said when Erin stepped into the yard.

"Me and the potato salad," she announced.

"Hayley will bring more barbecue sauce as soon as it's done."

Glory waved a dismissive hand. "I think they've forgotten about it already. But *you* haven't forgotten that Hayley and I want to talk to you about the wedding, have you?"

Erin answered with a shake of her head, although she didn't know why her suggestions or opinions would matter. She knew very little about weddings and nothing about double weddings. "I haven't forgotten. That's why I'm here." She laughed at the face Glory made. "Okay, that and being with family."

"We'll sneak off after we finish eating and put our heads together." Glory tipped her head to one side and smiled. "You know, you'll be next."

"Me? You must have me confused with somebody else."

Glory's eyes twinkled with mischief. "Oh, I don't think so." She looked toward the road, where headlights from a vehicle could be seen turning into the lane. "The last of the guests."

Jonah and Jake. Erin had made sure they'd been invited, and her brothers had seemed especially happy about it.

When the pickup came to the end of the lane and stopped, Dylan hurried over to the truck and opened the door. "I was wondering what was keeping you," he said as Jake climbed from it. "Good, I see you brought your new ranch hand with you."

Erin couldn't hear what Jake said, as Jonah rounded the front of the truck and joined them. After what she suspected were introductions, the three walked toward the house.

After Dylan introduced Jonah to Luke and Glory, Hayley stepped outside to join them with the barbecue sauce in her hands. Luke took the bowl from her and kissed her cheek. "Thanks, honey," he said. "I guess I should have told you earlier that it took more than one little bowl."

"It wasn't a problem," she answered, smiling. She turned to Jonah. "So you're the new wrangler we've been hearing about. How do you like working at Jake's ranch?"

"It's good," Jonah answered, and looked to Erin.

"He's a fast learner," Erin said with a smile for Jonah.

"A lot like Jake," Dylan added. "He was as green as he could be, but look at him now, a successful rancher."

Jonah looked at Jake. "I have two great teachers."

"Think you'll stay around?" Luke asked.

With a glance at Erin, then Jake, Jonah shrugged. "All I have is the summer, but I'll be back next year, if they'll have me."

Jake smiled at him. "Whenever you can make it, there's a job open for you."

Erin smiled, too, but didn't say anything. If everything went as she hoped, she would be back racing barrels by next summer. But nobody needed to know that. Not yet. Not until she had MacDuff trained to perfection and the money she needed. Until then, she would continue working for Jake.

Luke put a hand on Jonah's shoulder. "Erin will find a way to make sure there's a spot for you. She's stubborn that way."

"Stubborn?" she asked, planting her hands on her hips and scowling at him. "There's no one more stubborn than you two."

"Except Jake," Dylan added. "He said he'd be back, and he is."

Jake held up both hands. "Hey, I didn't plan it, but it worked out. And talking about work, this house has had a lot of work done on it. I hardly recognized it."

"You haven't seen the best part," Dylan said. "Come inside and see what Glory did with it."

Hayley turned around. "Where's Brayden?"

"Right here," Jake answered.

Brayden stood in front of Jonah, staring up at him. "Jake," he said, and everyone laughed.

Jonah shook his head with a small smile, as Luke corrected the mistake. "That's Jonah," Luke said. "Jonah, this is my son, Brayden."

Jonah leaned down. "Hi, little buddy. Do you like horses, too?"

Nodding, Brayden glanced at Jake, then back again at Jonah. "Jo-*nah,*" he said, grinning. "Wanna ride a horse?"

"You bet," Jonah answered. "Maybe in a few days?"

"Yeah!"

Dylan motioned for everyone to follow. "Time for a tour."

Luke offered to keep an eye on the ribs, and Hayley said she would keep him company, but the others followed Dylan into the house. Erin waited to be the last one inside. She'd been in the house a thousand times but still felt odd about everything that had changed. Not that she didn't like it. She loved it. But it sometimes reminded her how much she missed her parents, and she hoped they were proud of who she and her brothers had become.

"Wow," she heard Jake say as she stepped into the kitchen. He turned to Glory. "You did this?"

Laughing, Glory nodded. "With help. What do you think?"

Jake turned around in a circle, looking at everything. "If you'd blindfolded me and brought me in, I wouldn't have known where I was, but it's great. Really great."

Dylan led them through the rest of the house, then upstairs, and Glory explained the work that had been done. Jake listened carefully, asking questions, obviously impressed.

"I didn't know so much could be done with a house this old. It's almost like new but still has the charm that I remember as a kid. What do you think, Jonah?"

Busy playing a game of hide-and-seek with Brayden, Jonah turned to look at him. "I don't know what it looked like before, but it's really nice. Comfortable, you know?"

"That's it," Jake said. "As comfortable as it always was, but updated. It's great, Glory. You really know your stuff."

Glory thanked him and they started down the stairs. Erin noticed that Jake hung back, studying some of the smaller changes that had been made.

When everyone else had gone, he turned to her. "So what do you think? Lots of changes to the place where you grew up."

"I like it," she answered honestly. Leaning back against the stair railing, she let her gaze travel the upstairs foyer. "I don't regret hiring Glory one bit. She's done a wonderful job, and I know my parents would be as proud of it as we all are."

Facing her, he took her hand in his. "But it's hard, isn't it?" he asked, his voice soft and caring.

She nodded. "Sometimes. I miss them. I've never stopped."

Silent for a moment, he moved a little closer. "Did you miss *me,* Erin?"

She didn't want him to see how his question affected her, so she kept her head lowered. "I tried not to."

With his other hand, he lifted her chin with a finger. "You've done well. You should be proud. I know your parents are."

He leaned closer for what she knew would be a kiss, but she saw movement in the stairwell. Jonah stood at the bottom of the stairs, watching them, with a strange expression on his face.

"They said to let you know the food is ready," he said, then disappeared.

"Don't worry about him," Jake said.

But she did. Something seemed odd, but she couldn't put a finger on what it might be.

JAKE LEANED BACK in the patio chair and sighed. "Now, that's what I call *barbecue.* Have you two thought about opening up a place of your own? It's that good."

Dylan shook his head. "No time for that kind of thing."

"He's right," Luke said. "We keep busy enough and the ranch is doing well. Barbecuing is something we do for enjoyment."

"Relaxation," Dylan corrected. "We don't do it often enough to get tired of it. Glory and Hayley seem to enjoy it, too."

"Something to share with them," Jake said, not realizing he'd spoken. "You have pretty much everything a man could want. A successful business, great women in your lives, and you, Luke, a son."

Dylan nodded, his expression serious in the bright yard light. "We've been lucky. For a while there, I didn't think—"

"It's all good," Luke reminded him. "I hate to say it, but that sister of ours knows how to pick the right women. She should set up a matchmaking business for men who don't realize they want a wife."

"Not a bad idea, considering how happy you

two are," Jake said. "She did a good job with you." He didn't have that problem. He'd found Erin again. Now he faced the problem of convincing her that he hadn't meant to break her heart.

The sound of the screen door opening and closing caused all three of them to look in that direction to see Jonah coming down the stone steps.

"Grab a chair," Luke told him, and pointed to one at the side of the house.

Jonah picked up the chair and carried it over to set it beside Jake and settled on it. "Brayden was wound up but so worn out that he went to sleep still talking."

"He's a go-getter," Luke said, smiling. "I was just thinking about the time Hayley showed up here for the nanny job." He turned his focus on Jake. "Just one of Erin's little schemes."

"She mentioned something about it," Jake said.

"She's the one who found Hayley. A niece

of somebody Erin knew from the circuit. As usual, Erin wouldn't take no for an answer, and before I knew it, Hayley was standing on my doorstep. Brayden took to her immediately, when before he wouldn't have anything to do with anybody else, except Dylan."

Dylan, seated next to him, grunted. "He knew a good thing when he saw it. And then she hired Glory—without my permission—to redecorate this house. Look what that got me."

"What?" Jake asked. "A great house and an even better woman?"

Dylan's mouth stretched with a smile. "Exactly."

"Like I said earlier," Luke said, "you have to be careful with Erin. If she wants something bad enough—even for somebody else—she'll get it done, no matter what."

"I couldn't have said it better," Dylan said.

"Jonah," Luke said, "Dylan and I have something we want to ask you."

Looking from Dylan to Luke to Jake, he answered, "Me?"

Jake didn't know what might be going on. Neither Dylan nor Luke had mentioned anything to him, and he had to admit he was curious. "Do you want me to leave?" he asked the brothers.

"No," Luke answered. "You need to know we're not sneaking around behind your back."

Unsure of what they were talking about, he nodded and waited.

Jonah cleared his throat. "What do you want to ask me?"

Dylan leaned forward. "You like ranch work?"

"Yeah," Jonah answered, glancing at Jake.

"We have a proposition for you," Dylan continued. "Would you be interested in giving us a hand next weekend? With Erin working at Jake's, we can use a third. But only if Jake can do without you for a day."

Jonah glanced at Jake, who nodded, before he

answered. “Yeah. Sure. If it’s okay with Jake. And Erin.”

“Erin doesn’t really have a say in it,” Jake pointed out, “but I’m sure she’d like to be in on the decision.”

Luke chuckled and looked at his brother before replying. “Sounds like Erin. Is she taking over your place, Jake?”

Jake had to laugh. Her brothers knew her well. “Not too much, but she does speak her mind.”

“She always has,” Dylan said. “Not that she doesn’t know what she’s talking about. Usually. But for some guys, it can be a pain to have a woman around who thinks she knows as much as he does.”

Jake agreed, except for one thing. “Sometimes she does know as much. But then I haven’t been at this ranching thing as long as the rest of you have. I’m still learning.”

Dylan nodded. “We all are.” He pushed out of his chair and stood. “I need to go check on a new calf in the barn. Would you like to come along, Jonah?"

Jonah shot to his feet. "Sure."

"I'll come, too," Luke said, standing. "What about you, Jake?"

"You all go on. I'll sit here and enjoy the evening, then check on the girls to make sure they aren't plotting something devious."

Luke picked up a flashlight from the ground. "If they are, take notes, then come get us."

Laughing, Jake watched them disappear in the dark, Luke leading the way with the light. Sitting alone, he thought about the things the Walker boys had said. They knew their sister better than most brothers would, but from what he could tell she'd never let on about what had happened between them. All he wanted now was to get back to where things had been before that night.

Standing, he went inside to the kitchen. He could hear the women's voices coming from the living room, but it was Erin's he heard more clearly.

"You two need to be the ones making the decision," she was saying. "I don't know nothin' 'bout havin' no weddin'."

Glory and Hayley laughed at her imitation. "You don't have to know about weddings," one of them answered. "Just tell us what you think will work and what won't."

Jake guessed it had been Glory who had spoken, but he couldn't be sure. *Wedding stuff.* He didn't know anything about it, either, so he and Erin were on level ground with that.

"We have to have two ministers," the other one said. "My dad insists that we have Reverend Fitzgerald, if he'll come this far. I'm sure he will, but won't he and Reverend Baker need to get together so they can plan the service?"

"Hayley," Erin said, "there's such a thing as a telephone."

"I know, but—" She laughed. "You're right. See? You are a big help. It's just that I talked to my mom this afternoon, and she was concerned. I guess I'm not thinking clearly."

Jake heard a soft grunt, and then Erin's voice. "I don't know how anyone can think, clearly or not, with all this stuff that has to be done just to get married."

A gasp drifted into the kitchen. "Erin Walker, haven't you ever thought about getting married?"

Glory had said it, Jake felt sure.

For a few seconds, he didn't hear anything, and then Erin answered. "Not really. Oh, maybe when I was a dreamy teenager, but, no, not that I recall all that clearly."

The other two women groaned, and Jake wondered if he might have been the object of Erin's dreams. It fit the right time. He didn't know of any other boy she'd given more than a thought to, and if she had—

"Now all we need is to know what kind of dress you want to wear, Erin. How simple can that be?"

"I have to wear a *dress?*"

"Oh, come on, Erin," Glory said. "You're kidding, right?"

"Mostly," Erin answered. "But I don't know why you two want to count on me so much. Even to be there. I don't know where I'll be next spring."

She what?

Before he could figure out what she might have meant, Hayley spoke. "We would have done this last spring, but with the new hospital dedication and opening, we decided to postpone it. Even so, you've always been the only one we want as our maid of honor."

"We each have a bridesmaid," Glory explained, "but we agreed to share you. It's the only thing we insist upon. And let's face it, Dylan and Luke aren't going to let you leave again."

He heard a sniff and knew it had come from Erin.

"I haven't made any plans to leave, so calm down."

"Good," Glory said, "because we aren't going to let you. You're going to be our maid of honor, and that's all there is to it. Now let's take a look at some of the dresses. Let me find that page.... Here it is."

Jake let go of the breath he'd been holding. No plans. She had no plans. Well, he did, and she would soon learn what they were. He wouldn't let her get away again, and he would for damn sure let her know how he felt about her.

Turning, he walked to the door, ready to leave as quietly as he'd arrived. But when he pushed open the door that led to the porch, the hinges groaned.

"Dylan?" Glory called.

Damn. He had to find a way to make it appear that he was coming in, not going out. He took a deep breath. "No, it's me. Jake. I came in to get—" He looked around and spied the refrigerator as she stepped into the kitchen. "A beer," he said in a rush. "Dylan mentioned there were more in there." He pointed to the refrigerator.

"I'll get one for you," she said.

While she pulled a bottle from the refrigerator, Hayley and Erin walked into the room. "What's going on?" he asked.

"Wedding plans," Hayley answered.

Glory handed him the beer. "We're trying to get Erin to pick out a dress."

"A dress?" he said, as if he didn't know anything that had been said. "I don't believe I've ever seen her in one. Make sure I get an invitation to this wedding."

Glory looked at Hayley, who smiled at her as she replied, "Oh, we will. You can count on it."

"Good. I'll be there with bells on."

The way Glory had looked at Hayley told him a lot. He had allies. He felt relieved. He might need them.

JONAH SKIMMED THE LETTER. He'd read it so many times that he'd memorized every word. But reading it gave him hope that what he had to do would be good for everyone.

Carefully folding it, he shoved it into his back pocket. He would wait until the right time, and then he would do what he came to do.

He closed the door of the bunkhouse behind him and stepped out into what promised to be another "scorcher of a day," as his dad always said. Crossing the yard to start a new day of work, he spied Jake standing by the barn.

"Good morning, Jonah," Jake called to him.

"I think it will be," he answered.

Jake laughed. "Once you're awake, huh?"

Jonah stopped and shaded his eyes. "I'm already there. Been up for an hour." Pulling out the sunglasses he'd bought in town, he slipped them on.

"Go on up to the house," Jake said. "Ada is waiting with pancakes for you."

Jonah waved as he walked to the house, his stomach rumbling. "Thanks. I'll do that." The day already felt perfect, even with the heat.

Opening the door, he heard the sound of frying bacon and recognized the smell of fresh pancakes and coffee. "Sure smells good," he said, when he stepped inside.

Ada turned from the stove, a spatula in one hand and a smile on her face. "I've been waiting for you. Grab a seat over there. I have some pancakes ready for you."

"My favorite," he said, settling on one of the high stools at the counter. "Have you seen Erin?"

"Not yet," Ada said over her shoulder, "but I 'spect she'll be here before long. Pancakes are her favorite, too, and I'd bargain she'll figure it out, the closer she gets to this ranch."

Jonah nodded. He and Erin had a lot in common. All three of them did—him, Erin and Jake. He still couldn't believe his luck that first day when Jake had hired him. He'd never thought that would happen. But it had, and no matter what, he would never forget it.

Hearing a noise, he turned around and saw Ada squirting whipped cream on top of a stack of pancakes. "How'd you know?"

"That's the way she always liked them," she said, spooning strawberries on top of the cream. "And you kind of remind me of her."

His interest kicked up. "How's that?"

"Jake told me about how you showed up one day, all eager and full of yourself, and—"

"Full of myself?" he asked. He'd been scared to death, especially not knowing if he'd found the right place. But he'd learned then that determination made people do things they wouldn't usually do.

"No, I don't mean what you're thinkin'," Ada replied. "You were confident, I guess you'd say. That's the way I remember Erin when she was a girl. Nothing kept her down, not even when things took a bad turn."

He wanted to know more. "Bad turn?"

She put the plate down in front of him. "When her folks died. They were the world to her, and she was like a lost lamb, but she didn't stay that way for long. She stepped right up and did what needed to be done. She took care of those boys, just like her mama had, until Luke finished school. Then she took off for the rodeo and made her own life."

He learned something new about Erin every day and didn't think he could've done the same. Cutting off the first bite of pancake, he lifted the fork to his mouth, and then realized he'd done something similar. He'd done what he wanted and left home, made it to Desperation and found the person he'd come looking for. How many guys his age, not yet out of high school, would have done it? In spite of their parents telling them to leave it alone.

The first bite of pancake was fantastic, and he let Ada know how good it was and how much he appreciated it. Good manners had been something that had been drilled into him. Shoot, even his teachers mentioned how good his were.

When he finished his breakfast, he stood and rinsed his plate in the sink. "Thanks, Ada. Those were some dee-licious pancakes. Better than what you can get in a restaurant, that's for sure."

"Glad you enjoyed them, Jonah," she answered.

The door opened and Erin walked in. "Hey, Jonah," she greeted him. "Jake's looking for you. The others just arrived, so we'd better get to work. Jake's cracking the whip to get us all moving before it gets really hot."

He walked to the door and grinned at her. "We sure don't want to disappoint the boss."

Jake kept them all busy. With a chance of a storm later in the day, there were things to do before it hit. Jonah did the job Jake gave him, cleaning out stalls and putting in fresh hay and feed. When he finished that, Gary took him out to one of the far pastures, and they brought some of the cattle up closer to the house.

"We don't need to slog through mud, if this storm is as bad as they say it might be," Gary told him. "Jake likes to keep his livestock close at times like these. Electric fences have a tendency to short out in a windstorm if something blows up against them. Worse if the power goes out."

Jonah, getting impatient for the day to be over and everyone gone, tried to keep his mind on his work, instead of what he had to do later. The day went faster that way, so when the other wranglers said their goodbyes and left, he was ready.

He almost missed his chance, but he caught Erin as she started walking for home. Jake, as usual, stood near the corral, watching her start for the Walker ranch.

"Hey, Erin," Jonah called to her. "Do you have a minute?"

She stopped and turned around. "I don't want to get caught in the storm," she said, pointing at the dark clouds that were rolling in.

"It won't take long," he promised. Besides, if the storm came in when they were talking, he knew Jake would take her home.

"What's up?" Jake asked him while Erin retraced her steps.

"Just something for Erin," he answered. "You, too."

"Okay," Jake replied. "But make it quick. That storm is moving in fast."

They waited until Erin joined them, then Jonah took a deep breath, before speaking. "First, I want to thank both of you for giving me this job and letting me stay here. It's been an experience I never thought would happen."

Erin looked at Jake, who shrugged. "You've been a good addition to the group, Jonah," Jake said. "Eager to learn, doing whatever needs to be done. Nobody can ask much more than that."

"A stroke of luck for all of us," Erin said.

Jonah saw worry in her eyes. Something like he saw in his mom's when he asked to go do something she wasn't sure would be a good idea. His dad got the same look, too, when they'd talked about how much he wanted to get a job on a ranch. The only way he'd known his dad wasn't mad was that look in his eyes. *Concern,* people called it. Concern for others. But it hadn't been there when he'd shown them what he'd found and told them that he knew they'd lied to him. Not just for a while, but forever. That's why he'd left without telling them. He'd lied, too, but only because that was what they deserved.

Ready to do what he'd dreamed of doing for almost a year, he reached into his back pocket and pulled out the folded letter, then handed it to Erin.

"What's this?" she asked, looking at it, then at him.

"Something I thought you'd want to see. Both of you."

She glanced at Jake as if asking what he thought. He answered with a shrug. "Go ahead," he said. "Let's see what it is."

Jonah realized he was holding his breath, so he did his best to breathe and tried to relax. He'd imagined this moment a hundred times, even down to how surprised they would be. Watching her, he saw Erin's hands tremble a little, and he wondered what she thought it might be. Not bad news, he wanted to say.

She unfolded the two pages and looked at them. Her head came up, and she stared at him, her face white and her eyes wide. "Where did you get this?" she whispered.

"In a box of my stuff that my mom put up in the attic."

"When?"

He shrugged but had a feeling this wasn't going to go the way he'd hoped it would. "About a year ago."

Jake peered over her shoulder. "What is it?"

"Nothing," she said, and pressed the letter to her chest. "I'll tell you later. Jonah and I…we need to talk."

Jake glanced at Jonah and moved to stand beside Erin, holding out his hand. "He said it was for both of us."

She pressed the papers closer. "Jake, wait.

I—" She let go when he started to pull them from her, and she looked at Jonah with tears in her eyes, but he could tell she was trying to smile.

Jake started reading. His face got pale in what little was left of the sunshine, hiding behind the clouds, and then it slowly started to get red. He looked at Erin, his eyes narrowed. "What does this mean?" he asked, pointing at the letter.

"It means—"

"It means I'm your son," Jonah said. "Both of yours."

Erin reached for the letter. "I can explain, Jake."

Her hand froze inches from the letter as he looked at her, his eyes angry and cold. "Damn right you will." When she didn't answer, he added, "Right now."

Jonah suddenly realized he hadn't done it the right way. But now that the truth was out, he wouldn't take it back.

Chapter Seven

"Go on up to the house, Erin," Jake ordered, checking the sky. "I'll be there in a minute."

Erin couldn't move. She'd never thought this would happen. Never thought she would ever see the son she gave up. Never dreamed Jake would find out. And she didn't know what to do or say. Not until she heard what Jake had to say, and she didn't look forward to that.

"Come on, Erin," Jonah said, sounding as unsure as she felt.

Jake whipped around. "No, just Erin. I'll talk to you later."

Jonah's chin went up. "I have every right to be there, too. You can't stop me."

She realized how much he sounded like her. "Let him come, too, Jake. I want to know how he found my letter."

"So you did write it," he said.

"I never said I didn't."

He hesitated, watching both of them. "Okay, go with Erin. I want to see how bad this storm might get, and then the three of us will have a talk."

Jonah nodded and started walking toward the house, but Erin still couldn't seem to move. *Scared.* She'd only been scared twice. The first when she'd realized she was pregnant, and the second when the sheriff had come to tell her that her parents had been in an accident.

"Erin?"

She knew she had to start moving, do something. They had to get this done and over with. The time of reckoning had come. Walking silently next to the boy who she now knew was hers, she couldn't think of anything to say. Numb with shock and fear, it was as if she'd lost the power to think. She'd considered denying she'd written the letter, but she'd been so blindsided by it that she couldn't speak. What could she say to make things right?

Nothing.

Forcing herself to move, she followed Jonah inside. "Living room is that way," he said.

She shook her head. She'd never been farther than the kitchen to talk to Ada, and the thought of going anywhere else made her feel out of place. "We'll wait for Jake."

They stood in silence for what seemed like forever. Her nerves were stretched as far as possible, and she found breathing a problem. Finally, when she thought she would pass out, she took a deep breath.

Jonah cleared his throat. "I'm sorry, Erin. I thought he knew."

Swallowing and hoping words would come, she shook her head. "No, and I never planned to tell him."

"Why not?"

"Yeah, why not?"

She spun around to see Jake standing in the open doorway. "Because I never expected to see you again."

His face hardened. "Not good enough, Erin. And why should I believe he's mine?"

She gasped at his insinuation. He knew she'd been a virgin. He'd wanted to wait, but she hadn't.

"I'm not eighteen," Jonah said, before Erin could think of an answer to Jake's question. "I'm sixteen, almost seventeen. Next month."

Erin could see the quick calculation in Jake's eyes and the moment he accepted it. "Don't blame Jonah for this," she told him. "He's only the product of—"

"Don't say it," Jake snapped. He turned to Jonah. "What about your parents? Do they know you're here?"

Jonah's eyes narrowed, and he clenched his fists at his side. "They know I'm at a ranch in Oklahoma. That's all they need to know."

"Jonah!" Erin cried, thinking of how his parents must feel.

Jake gave her a warning glance. "Why's that, boy?"

"They never told me I was adopted. When I found the letter, they tried to deny it. My dad, mostly. I could tell my mom wanted to tell me. I think she tried to a few times but never did."

"I'm sure they had their reasons," Erin said, wondering what she would have done in the same situation. But she knew she would have told the child the moment she held him. Still, she couldn't blame them, but she'd never expected he would come looking for her. She'd only hoped the couple who had adopted him had loved him. And she felt sure they had.

"So you got mad at them?" Jake asked.

Jonah faced him. "Wouldn't you have?"

Jake opened his mouth to answer, and then shut it to frown at both of them. "It doesn't matter what I would have done. It's what Erin did—and didn't do—that concerns me."

"You don't care?" Jonah asked, his voice rising. "You don't care if the people I thought were my parents have lied to me all my life?"

"I think you need to sit down and have a talk with your parents," Jake said. "And I think you should have said something that first day you walked up here, looking for a job. Basically, you lied to me." He glanced at Erin. "To both of us."

Jonah shook his head. "I couldn't tell you. I didn't know for sure. Look at the letter again. All I had were the initials *E.W.* No name, no place, no nothing. I might have been wrong, and then look at the mess it would have made."

"It's a mess now," Jake pointed out. He closed his eyes, sighed and then opened them. "Look, I know what it's like to be angry at someone who wants to keep you from what you want, but running away doesn't help. It only makes things worse."

"They wouldn't tell me anything," Jonah said in a belligerent tone.

Erin felt she needed to explain. "Maybe they didn't know anything they *could* tell you." He gave her a puzzled look. "Jonah, there's no information given to either the adoptive parents about the mother or to the mother about them. Not unless that's the way the adoption is set up from the beginning. Yours wasn't one of those."

He stared at her. "You're saying you never wanted to know me?"

She shook her head. "No, that's not what I'm saying. I was too young to raise a baby. I couldn't do it on my own. I had school to finish and a dream to chase." She dropped her gaze. "Maybe that's selfish—"

"I'm not blaming you. Just them."

"But they did what they thought was right, the same as I did."

"Well, it wasn't."

His mulish expression reminded her of herself at his age. She hoped she could change the way he felt about his parents not being open with him. "How did you find us, Jonah? With only two initials and nothing more, I can't think of how it happened."

He gave a jerky shrug. "It just happened."

"I can't accept that."

Jake took a step toward them. "Maybe I should call your parents and—"

"Don't!" Jonah closed his eyes and shook his head. "Please. I'll tell you. But the thing is…I don't want to get my friend in trouble."

"Friend?" Erin asked. Who would have known? Only her parents, and they'd been gone for fifteen years. Her brothers knew nothing. She'd made sure of that. Ada knew. She'd helped her get through it, but she never would have told anyone. "You don't have to mention any names. No one will be in trouble."

He seemed to consider it, and then nodded slowly. "One of my friends knows your aunt."

Erin gasped. "Aunt Janelle told you?"

He shook his head. "No, but she mentioned you to one of her good friends, my friend's grandmother. My friend was there when she said that her niece from Oklahoma had stayed with her one summer and had a baby she gave up. The dates fit." He shrugged again, more easily this time. "When I showed the letter to my friend, she told me what she overheard."

"But you didn't have any names, so how could you know who to look for?"

"Search for," he said. "That's what it's called. Searching. And I did have something. I had the name of the town. Desperation. My friend remembered it because it was, well, different."

Erin didn't know whether to be angry with her aunt or thank her. "Still, no name."

"It's a small town, and your aunt had said you lived outside of town on a ranch." His eyes brightened. "I knew then why I'd always wanted to learn to ride."

Jake grunted. "That's hard to believe. Too easy." Both of them looked at him, and he lifted one shoulder.

"It wasn't easy," Jonah argued. "It took a long time. Almost a year."

"So you came to Desperation looking for Erin?"

"I came looking for a girl with the initials *E.W.*, but I didn't know her name. I did a lot of research," Jonah admitted. "I have my own computer, and my friend and I spent hours looking through everything we could find about Desperation and the ranches in the area. I still didn't have a name. There are several people with a last name that starts with a *W.* But I decided to come and find out whatever I could. A friend—a different one—was on his way to visit family in Texas, and he agreed to drop me off in Desperation."

"How did you find *this* ranch," Jake asked, "or know who to look for?"

Jonah smiled. "I saw an ad in a ranching magazine. The first place I stopped was the Chick-a-Lick Café, and I saw the flyer there, too. I asked a few questions and figured that I might be able to find out something by stopping by.

It was luck that you asked if I'd come about the job."

"And then you lied about your age."

"It seemed like the smart thing to do, until I could find Erin. Not that I thought I would. I couldn't believe it when you introduced her. Erin Walker. E.W."

Erin shook her head, amazed how everything had fallen together. "And then you asked me a lot of questions."

"I had to know to make sure you were the one I was looking for." He looked at Jake. "It took me longer to figure out that you're my—"

"That has yet to be determined."

Erin stared at Jake, unable to believe that he couldn't accept that they had a son. She could understand that he'd been surprised—no, shocked. But did he really need to deny that he might have fathered a son?

Too angry and confused, she turned and started for the kitchen. "I'm going home."

As if on cue, a loud crack of thunder shook

the windows. "Go on to the bunkhouse, Jonah," Jake said. "Erin and I have some things to discuss. I'll see you in the morning."

"But—"

"Go on."

Even Erin could tell he wouldn't back down on it. But she didn't want to have the conversation she knew was coming if she stayed. "It's about to rain. I need to get home before it starts."

Jake turned to her with a look on his face she'd only seen once. "I'll make sure you get home dry and in one piece."

With no choice, she stayed where she was. Somehow, she would get through this.

"WHY DIDN'T YOU tell me?" he demanded, watching her closely.

"I never expected to see you again. I didn't have much of a choice. You weren't there."

He couldn't remember ever being this angry, not even at his parents. He took three steps toward her and looked down into her upturned face. "Don't blame this on me, Erin. All you had to do was—"

"You were long gone by the time I knew." Color flooded her face, blotching her cheeks with red. "I didn't know what to do. I was scared. I did the best I could."

"For you, maybe." Hadn't she given any thought to him? "Who knows about this?"

"Me," she answered. "Only me. Not even Dylan and Luke know. I went to stay with my mother's sister in Kansas that summer before my senior year. No one in Desperation even guessed why. Except Ada."

"Ada? My cook?"

Erin nodded. "Somehow I fooled everyone except her. She helped me make the decision but never told me what I should do, only held me when I cried. I had him—the baby—and signed the papers to relinquish him for adoption. I never saw him, never held him."

But she'd had an option. "You could have

gone to Uncle Carl. He would have gotten in touch with me."

"And you would have done what?" she demanded. "Rushed back here? Would you have even believed me? Would you have cared? You didn't when—"

"You didn't even try!" he shouted. "You didn't give one thought to me or what I might have wanted."

Her eyes blazed with anger. "And you gave how much thought to what I wanted?"

If only she knew, but he wouldn't tell her. He didn't know if she deserved to know why he'd broken it off with her. "Stop excusing it," he said, his fury building. "You were the one who—"

"Seduced you?" The smile she gave him was hard and brittle. "I did. I admit it. Put the blame on me. I don't care."

His head hurt, his heart even more. It came down to one thing. One, simple thing. Taking her by the arms, he pulled her to within inches of him. "No more excuses, Erin," he said, saying each word louder until he shouted, "Why didn't you tell me?"

She stiffened in his hands and met his gaze. "You lost the right to know when you walked out on me that night."

"The hell I did!" Releasing her, he stepped back, breathing hard.

"It's exactly what you did," she shouted back at him. "You threw me away, told me it was over between us. After we'd— You told me, in no uncertain terms, that you were leaving to go back to college in the morning and you wouldn't be back. Ever."

Shaking his head, he answered, "You don't know what you're talking about."

"I know exactly what I'm talking about. I've never forgotten it." She took a step back. "Take me home. I want to go home. Now."

He felt the walls closing in on him. He hadn't wanted to leave her, but he hadn't been given a choice. His parents decided he would go to college, not become a rancher. It wasn't what they'd planned for him. He still wondered why the one thing he'd wanted had never mattered to them.

"It's raining," he said, pointing at the windows streaked with rain.

"Now."

He wouldn't keep her there against her will. "Okay. But this isn't finished."

"Yes, it is."

They didn't speak a word on the short drive to the Walker ranch, where there'd been very little rain, if any. He drove up the lane and past the barn, bringing the truck to a stop within a few yards of her RV. She opened the door and jumped out, not even giving him a chance to say anything. But what could he say? He *had* ended it with her. But it hadn't been as much for himself as it had been for her.

Back home, he stripped down and climbed into bed, his head throbbing, as the words they'd said to each other repeated over and over.

He barely slept, and when the sun came up in the morning, he still didn't know how he felt, except for being confused and hurt.

When Erin didn't show up for work an hour after the others started their day, he began to worry. Maybe they would never get this figured out. He owed her an explanation, but he didn't know how to do it or even if he should try. Did it matter now? He didn't think it did. And she might not believe him.

"Do you think she left?" Jonah asked, another hour later, as they led the horses out of the barn.

"I don't know," he admitted. But he *needed* to know. "I'll go check on her."

"But if she isn't there—"

"I'll talk to her brothers if she isn't. If she is, I don't think she'd mention to them that something happened. If she decided to leave, she'd just…leave."

"She might not tell you or her brothers," Jonah said, "but she'd tell me. I know she would."

"Maybe," Jake said. *And maybe not.*

Twenty minutes later, he arrived at the Walker ranch to find Erin working with MacDuff in the corral—a sure sign she had things on her mind she didn't want to think about.

Not wanting to spook her or her horse, he stayed far enough away to see and hear, but made sure he didn't appear to be hiding. No need to give her more reason to be angry. He needed to talk to her. But first, he wanted to see if the training had progressed.

It didn't take long to realize there'd been a lot of changes, both in her horse and in her. Instead of losing her temper, she spoke gently but firmly. MacDuff took the barrels as if he'd been born to do it. No hesitation as he rounded the first and the others. Erin had found whatever had been missing.

When she finished the last round, Jake approached the corral. "I knew you could do it," he said as he reached the fence.

When she looked up, her wide-eyed gaze met his. Apparently she hadn't seen him watching her. Neither a smile nor a frown appeared on her face. "Thanks to you," she said.

It took him by surprise. "What did I do?"

She busied herself with the saddle cinch. "You made me think, and I realized…I guess I've been too eager and expected too much from a horse that I didn't want to hold a candle to Firewind."

"You would have figured it out."

"And I would have told you about having your baby."

He didn't know whether to believe her or not. "But you said—"

"I know what I said," she stated simply, keeping her attention on her horse and saddle. "I never planned to tell you. I never expected to see you again. I never expected to see our son, either."

She made it sound so simple. He saw the simplicity, too, but in a different way. By not telling him, she'd lied. He didn't know if he could ever forgive her for that.

He wondered how she'd managed to do what she'd done—give away a child. Their child. "Did it get easier?" he asked.

Her hands stilled and she turned her head to look at him. "If you think I'm going to say it was, you're wrong. It didn't get easier. I found a way to keep it from being uppermost in my mind, but it would sneak in when I least expected, and then it felt like hitting a wall at high speed." Her hands dropped to her sides and she faced him. "It hurt, Jake. All of it. And I know you hurt, too, right now. But I can't take it back. I can't undo what I did."

He couldn't fight her. It would only make it harder for all of them. Worse, he couldn't change what had happened. They had to move forward. But in which direction?

"Jonah was afraid you'd quit," he finally said.

"My job?"

He nodded. He didn't want her to leave. But he didn't know how he would be able to see her every day and act as if nothing had happened.

"It's up to you, Jake," she said without looking at him. "If you don't want me around, say so. I'll find something else."

Unable to answer, he stood, watching her. He'd loved her for so long, he didn't know if he could stop. And he did still love her, but it was buried in his anger and her betrayal. If he could get past that…

"You didn't come to work today," he said, "so he thought—and so did I—that you'd left. That's why I'm here."

She grabbed the saddle with both hands but didn't remove it from MacDuff. "Where would I go?"

He knew exactly where she'd go. "Back to rodeo."

She slowly turned her head to study him. "It served me well when I needed it the most."

"Will it again?"

She hesitated, then shrugged and pulled the heavy saddle toward her.

"Erin?" he asked, worried and afraid to hear her answer but knowing he needed to.

"I don't know, Jake. Things have changed, now that I know who Jonah is."

She had changed. Overnight. She'd lost her spark, and he couldn't be sure what she might do. They'd both been angry the night before, and he still hadn't gotten over it. And now she'd left it up to him. But they still had one thing in common. Jonah.

"He's only here for the summer," he said, as much to himself as to her.

"If that," she answered.

At first, he didn't understand what she meant. "You think he'll leave now?"

"I don't know what he'll do." She set the saddle on the ground and removed the saddle blanket from MacDuff.

He wondered how it had been for her, to give up their baby. To carry him for nine months, and then give him up. "You never saw him after he was born?"

She shook her head. "I couldn't. Seeing him would have meant..." She shook her head again. "But there's one thing I do know."

"What's that?"

"He needs to call his parents."

Jake hadn't thought of that. Typical Erin, thinking of others and how they might feel. "You're probably right."

"I know I am."

He watched as she picked up the saddle blanket and took it into the barn. He waited until she returned for the saddle. "I'll get that for you."

Bending down, she looked over her shoulder. "I'm a big girl now, Jake. I can do my own work. But thanks for the offer."

They were back at square one. Polite. No, they were in a place he didn't know. Not with Erin. Not the Erin he knew. Would that sass come back? Did he want it to? Could he walk away and never look back? He'd been looking back for so long, it wouldn't be easy not to.

Questions were all he had. No answers. And

he needed answers, if only to help him move out of this hole of not knowing what to do or say.

"Come to work tomorrow, Erin," he said without thinking. "We'll talk to Jonah in the morning, tell him to call his parents and let them know where he is."

"And who he's with." With a grunt, she jerked the saddle from the ground and walked on to the barn.

Who he's with. He'd been so wrapped up in his own feelings, he hadn't given any thought to the two people who'd raised his son. He owed them an explanation and his thanks. He and Erin both did.

He climbed over the fence and met her at the door to the barn. "You'll come to work tomorrow, then?"

"Less questions to answer from the others if I do."

She had a point. "Yeah, that's true," he said. Somehow they would have to keep the other cowboys from seeing that anything had changed. "But can we—"

"We don't have a choice."

Another good point. She'd known exactly what he'd been thinking. They would have to talk to Jonah before the others arrived.

"Come a little early," he told her, ready to go back and tell Jonah she hadn't gone. "I won't say anything to Jonah about calling his parents until you're there."

"All right. Now can I get my horse?"

For a second, he didn't know what she meant, and then he remembered she'd left MacDuff in the corral. Erin never put a horse away without giving it a good grooming.

"Sure," he said, backing away. "I'll see you in the morning."

Her mouth turned up in a smile, but her eyes were dull. Empty. "I'll be there with bells on."

He doubted they would be ringing for him.

"GIVE IT YOUR BEST. Don't let him get the upper hand, and don't let him get to you," Erin said to herself on her way to Jake's ranch the next morning. It wasn't all about her and Jake, it involved Jonah and his parents, too. If she and Jake worked together, they could make a difference.

When she came to the corral on the near side of the ranch, she checked to make sure the other wranglers hadn't arrived and spied Jake on the porch. She didn't see Jonah.

Crossing to the house, she stepped onto the porch, where he sat with a cup of coffee.

"I wasn't sure you'd come," he answered, buttering a piece of toast.

His lack of trust in her hurt. But she wouldn't let him know how much. "Then you don't know me as well as you think you do. I don't walk out on people."

He put down the knife and toast and looked at her. "But you think I walked out on you."

She shook her head. "I didn't mean that, but think whatever you like. Is Ada here yet?"

"She'll be here soon."

"I didn't know she would be cooking breakfast, too."

"I didn't plan on it, but she asked if she could. I'd be a fool to turn that down. She makes the best omelets and pancakes."

"She makes the best everything," Erin said. But she hadn't come early because of that. "Is Jonah up yet?"

"He's in the barn doing some chores I gave him." He pushed away from the table and stood. "So now we do what we planned."

"And that is…?"

"Call his parents."

She didn't feel comfortable doing that but followed him into the house. "We go behind his back? Why not let *him* call them?"

He stopped and turned back to look at her. "Because he wouldn't do it."

He continued through the kitchen and turned the corner into a room that appeared to be an office. "Why would you think that?" she asked.

Motioning to an empty chair, he stood behind

the desk. "Trust me, Erin. I've been there. Sixteen, seventeen, even eighteen, it doesn't matter. A guy that age will only tell his parents what he believes they want to hear."

"Isn't that pretty much any teenager?" she asked with a smile.

"Maybe. Probably," he relented, "but I'm speaking from personal experience."

The look he gave her had her wondering what he had told his own parents about his summers on his uncle's ranch. Had he ever mentioned her?

He pulled a paper out of his desk drawer. "I have their phone number, and I'm fairly sure they'll both be there this early in the morning. Jonah mentioned once that his dad is a banker. I don't think he meant to, but…bankers often work later hours, or at least those I've known do."

She stopped a sigh. It all seemed so cloak-and-dagger, and her conscience rebelled against it. "How did you get their number?"

"I took it from his phone. I'd say *Home* would mean just that, wouldn't you?"

She nodded slowly, wishing she knew how to tell him how much she didn't think they should do this. But she didn't want to argue. There'd been enough of that. "Which of us is going to do the talking?"

"Me."

"Maybe I should—"

"No," he answered before she could finish. "I've given it a lot of thought. It'll be fine."

She doubted it, but she didn't say so. "All right. But how will I know what they're saying?"

He opened another drawer. "With this," he said, handing her a cordless phone. "But put it on mute. Two of us talking at once might get confusing."

"If you say so," she replied but still didn't like it. At least she wouldn't be left out of the conversation.

"Let me dial, and when someone answers,

you turn on your phone." He waited until she nodded. "Okay. Are you ready?"

She nodded again.

Seconds ticked by, then Jake said, "Mrs. Butterfield?"

Erin turned on her phone, muted it and listened.

"Yes, this is Mrs. Butterfield."

"My name is Jake Canfield, ma'am. I own the ranch where your son Jonah is working."

She gasped, and quickly said, "Is Jonah all right?"

Erin smiled. She'd had a feeling Jonah's mother had a good heart. The woman's reaction convinced her of it.

"He's fine," Jake said. "I wasn't sure you knew exactly where he is, so I thought I should let you know."

In the background, Erin heard a man's voice and guessed it was Jonah's dad. Voices were suddenly muffled, and then someone spoke into the phone.

"Who is this?" the man said. When Jake repeated the information he'd given Mrs. Butterfield, the man grunted. "You're employing a minor. You know that, don't you?"

"Yes, that's why I'm calling," Jake answered. "Farms and ranches in Oklahoma can employ minors, but as I told your wife, I wasn't sure if you knew exactly where he is, and I wanted to assure you that he's fine and doing a great job."

Another grunt echoed over the lines. "Ranching," he said, as if it were a bad word. "I don't know where he got this crazy idea, but—"

"From me," Jake said. He glanced at Erin. "I think I understand where he's coming from. I was the same way, at his age."

"I don't see how that relates to—"

"Mr. Butterfield, I called—" He glanced at Erin. "Erin Walker is listening on another phone. We wanted to let you know that she's Jonah's—"

"Birth mother," Mrs. Butterfield said.

It was Erin's turn to gasp. She pushed the button to end the mute feature. "You knew?"

"I—I had a feeling," Jonah's mother said. "I don't know why, except that he was so angry with us and...well, I wondered if he hadn't found some information. Somehow."

Erin heard the sound of a disgusted sigh and guessed each of them were on phones, as she and Jake were. "He's a smart young man," she told them. "And maybe someday soon he'll explain to both of you how he found us."

"It doesn't matter how he found you," Mr. Butterfield said. "Put him on a bus and send him home. Today."

"Scott, please," his wife said. "Look how ingenious he was to do this. It isn't easy. He could have waited until he turned eighteen and requested his original birth certificate. That's how it's set up here in Kansas. But he didn't. And I don't blame him. I've been worried, yes, but he is a smart young man."

"He's a kid."

Jake made a face. "He's doing a fine job here, Mr. Butterfield," Jake said. "Can I call you Scott?"

Again, Erin heard muffled words, and then Scott Butterfield answered. "Yes, I guess you should. But who are *you?* If that woman is Jonah's…"

"Birth mother," his wife said. "That seems to be the proper term."

Jake cleared his throat. "Which makes me Jonah's birth father."

"A rancher."

"Yes, Scott, a rancher," Jake said. "Something I always wanted but was kept from it because my father was just like—"

"Jake, let me handle this," Erin interrupted. "Please?" She watched the battle he fought with himself, and then he nodded.

Before she could say anything to Jonah's parents, she heard his mother say, "Go on to work, Scott, or you'll be late. You have that meeting you can't miss this morning. We mothers will handle this. You're too emotional and upset, and you need some time to think."

Erin could have hugged her. She heard him say something, but couldn't make out what it was, and then she waited.

"Erin?" Jonah's mother said. "That's right, isn't it?" When Erin said it was, she continued. "I'm Christine, but call me Chris. I have a feeling we're going to become good friends."

"I hope so," Erin replied. "I hope we all will. But I want you to know that Jake and I didn't learn who Jonah was until two days ago. Believe me, it was a shock for both of us, so I can imagine how you must feel." She looked at Jake. "And Jake didn't know about Jonah at all until then, so—"

"Oh, my! That has to be—"

"Something to get used to," Jake said, then hung up the phone. "Erin, at least see if they'll let him stay a few more weeks. I'd like to spend some time with him, now that—"

"Tell Jake that I'll make sure his father doesn't insist he come home right now," Chris said.

So Jake would know it would be all right, Erin nodded. "Thank you, Chris. We all have a lot to learn."

"We sure do," Chris said, laughing. "Now tell me how you learned he's yours, too."

Chapter Eight

After checking on his men, who were arriving, and making sure Jonah kept busy, Jake returned to his office to find Erin still on the phone. She glanced at him with a smile, told Jonah's mother goodbye and turned to him.

"I think it's going to be all right," she said. "I hope I'll get to meet her someday."

Listening to her talk to Jonah and his mother, he'd begun to understand how she must have felt when she discovered she was pregnant. He could only imagine. He wasn't as angry now as he had been and admitted to himself that he had to accept some of the blame, too. It took two to make a baby. And she'd bore the brunt of it.

"She seemed nice," he answered, still reeling from everything that had happened. "But Scott is another matter."

She shook her head. "He's been worried. Apparently Jonah called them a few days after he arrived here, told them he had a job on a ranch in Oklahoma, but nothing more. He called two more times to let them know he was okay, but Chris said his tone had been belligerent. His dad isn't crazy about Jonah's 'preoccupation,' as he called it, with ranching. I explained it was natural."

That same strange feeling came over him again, the same one he'd felt when talking to Jonah's dad. Scott Butterfield reminded him of— "My dad was the same," he admitted.

"But he sent you here every summer."

He nodded, thinking of the years he'd had to beg his mother to help him convince his dad to let him go. "Thanks to my mother. Uncle Carl was her brother, but even so, my dad had a poor view of the country life."

"I remember you mentioning that he wasn't crazy about you being there, but I didn't realize... But it doesn't matter now, does it?"

He wondered if it did, but decided to leave all that behind. It wouldn't change anything. "No," he said, "it doesn't."

"You get along well with him now?" she asked.

He sat on the edge of the desk. "We get along okay, but I think he's a little disappointed that I didn't follow in his footsteps."

"Then I guess you can relate to how Jonah is feeling, at least in that respect. As for the other..."

She dipped her head, obviously to avoid looking at him. "I can't change anything, Jake. What's done is done."

He wanted to say what was in his heart, but he couldn't. His feelings were at war with each other, while she seemed calmer after talking to Jonah's mother.

"I shouldn't have been so hard on you," he

said, "but I've never been kicked in the head before. I think I have a clue what it must feel like." It was the closest he could get to an apology.

"I understand that," she said. "I hope you can find a way to forgive me someday."

"I'm trying, Erin. Maybe with a little more time…" Maybe everything would somehow work out for them. They'd weathered the storm. But where did they go from here?

At the sound of a throat clearing, she jumped back and he saw Jonah standing in the doorway. "Am I interrupting?" Jonah asked.

Jake glanced at Erin before answering. "Come on in, Jonah."

Jonah looked from one to the other. "I hope it's getting better. You know, between you." He seemed wary, obviously knowing he'd caused more trouble than he'd expected.

Jake looked at Erin again. "We're working on it. But we want to tell you something."

A glint of hope flashed in his eyes. "Good news, I hope."

"We think so." At least he did, and he thought Erin did, too. "But I'll let Erin tell you."

"We've spoken to your parents, Jonah," she began, "And—

"You *what?*" Jonah said, his voice louder than normal and his eyes wide. "How could you do that?"

"Because they needed to know exactly who you're with," she explained. "It's only fair."

His eyes narrowed. "Fair to who? They weren't fair to me when they didn't tell me I didn't belong to them."

Erin reached out to him, but he took a step back, and her hand fell to her side. "You *do* belong to them, Jonah. I gave you to them."

"They should have told me."

"Perhaps, but they had their reasons, whether you or I agree with them or not."

Jake listened and watched in awe of the way Erin handled it. He couldn't have done it so well. Her sass had been replaced with calm, something he didn't yet feel.

"How'd you find their phone number?" Jonah asked, angry red spots on his cheeks.

"I checked your cell phone," Jake admitted.

"That's my private property!"

Jake saw himself in his son. The anger, the feeling of betrayal. He'd known it, too, at the same age. "You're a minor," he reminded Jonah. "And you lied about your age, then admitted that you'd pretty much run away. I had no choice but to let your parents know you're here, doing well, and exactly who Erin and I are."

"But you didn't have the right—"

"You're living here under my care, Jonah," Jake said, taking a cue from Erin. He'd never forgive himself if he didn't handle this the right way. And he suddenly saw himself as his father. If they'd been able to talk, maybe things would have been different. But somewhere along the line, they'd quit talking.

Jonah's chin jutted out when he spoke. "And I suppose you're sending me back."

Erin answered, her voice soft and gentle. "No, you're staying here, as you planned, then returning before school starts."

Shaking his head, Jonah looked away. "I don't believe it. He'd never let me—"

"It's being taken care of," she told him.

Slowly, he turned his head to look at her. "Don't be too sure. My dad will come down here and get me. But I won't go back—"

"They may come for a visit in a few weeks," Erin said. "We haven't worked that out yet. But your mom assured me that they wouldn't make you come home." She smiled at him. "Trust me, Jonah, moms know how to make things happen." When he seemed to calm down, she continued. "You don't have any idea how worried they've been. If it had been me, I'd be half out of my mind."

Jonah stared at the floor. "I was mad," he mumbled, "and hurt."

She moved to him and put her arm around his shoulder. "We all have a bit of revenge in us. We're human. But trust me when I say that we—all of us—care about you and want you to be happy."

He raised his head to look at her. "And I can stay? You're sure?"

"Until the end of summer," she said, nodding.

Jake pushed to his feet. "But only if you get back to work. No goofing off. You don't get special treatment here."

"Right," Jonah answered. And then he seemed to relax. "You're right. I'd better go help Bobby Ray, and you two can get back to working it out."

Jake moved from the desk and gave him a fatherly pat on the back. "We all have jobs to do."

When Jonah had gone, he turned to Erin. "I just realized—you're a great mom, Erin," he whispered. "I wish—"

She sighed. "Savor the moment because it won't always be this easy."

"Easy?" He shook his head. "You mean it gets worse?"

"Much worse, believe me."

He didn't know how much worse he could take. The past few days had been a nightmare, and he didn't want to repeat it. He walked closer to her but didn't look at her. Stopping at his desk, he glanced down. On it, he saw the invitation that had arrived in the mail a few days earlier. He'd intended to ask Erin—

Dammit, he loved her. Even though he'd been blindsided when he'd learned Jonah was his son and furious at her for not telling him, he knew in his heart that he shared the blame. She'd kept something from him—something he might never have known if he hadn't come back—but he hadn't been honest with her, either. He wanted to make things right between them.

"Erin," he said, turning around to find her watching him, "would you go to the dance with me next week? Even your brothers said they'd get all gussied up for it."

Was it hope he saw in her eyes? He couldn't be sure, so he waited.

"The formal dance?" she asked. When he nodded, she hesitated. "I thought you'd never—Yes. I will."

ERIN STARED AT her reflection in the antique cheval mirror. The dress Glory had insisted she buy had Erin wondering if she'd lost her mind. She'd never worn anything like it.

Standing behind her, Glory smiled. "It's beautiful, Erin. I knew that dress would be perfect."

Pressing her lips together, Erin's gaze met Glory's in the mirror. "You're sure it's not too much?" She smoothed her hands down the black fabric that fit like a second skin. "I mean—"

"It's perfect." Glory turned her head and looked over her shoulder. "Don't you think so, Hayley?"

"I couldn't have said it better." She walked

across the room to stand next to Glory, catching Erin's eye in the mirror. "Absolutely perfect."

Glory and Hayley had insisted that they all get ready together for the formal dance at Hayley's apartment at the Commune, but they'd been given a special room for the occasion.

The dance was being held to celebrate the renovation of the Big Barn. It stood near the ancestral family mansion of Hettie Racine Lambert, town matriarch and great-great-granddaughter of Colonel George Racine, who had founded the town of Desperation in the late 1800s. Hettie had originally donated the home to use as the Shadydrive Retirement Home, where they were getting dressed, but everyone called it the Commune, and it now included apartments for anyone. Glory had been hired to do the renovations of the interior of the old, stone barn, so the night would be even more special for her, and Erin couldn't have been prouder to soon have her—and Hayley—as sisters-in-law.

Not only had Erin been invited to share in the

fun of getting ready for the dance, but Glory had helped pick out her dress, and then done magic on her hair and makeup. She barely recognized herself.

"Aren't we gorgeous?" Hayley, decked out in a green chiffon dress, asked.

"Dare I say it?" Glory replied, dressed in deep pink. "We look fabulous. That color is perfect on you, Hayley. It brings out the gold flecks in your eyes."

"Erin picked it out."

"You did?" Glory asked. When Erin nodded, Glory said, "See? You have great taste and a good eye for color."

A knock on the door prompted them all to turn around.

"Girls, there are three dashing men downstairs," Hettie said from the other side.

"Come in, Hettie," Glory called. "We need your final approval."

Opening the door, Hettie stepped into the

room. "Oh, heavens, girls, how beautiful you all look."

"Back at ya," Erin said with a wink. "That's a wonderful color for you."

Hettie preened and turned in a circle. "It makes me feel ten years younger. No, make that forty. I'm reminded of my first prom at Desperation High. But enough of that," she said with a wave of her hand. "Luke and Dylan and Jake are waiting downstairs. It's time for your grand entrances." She gave each one of them a careful hug, and then held on to Erin. "It's hard to imagine you racing barrels, you look so beautiful tonight."

The three younger women grabbed their clutches and started for the stairs. At the door, Hayley stopped to look back. "Hettie, you have a date, don't you?"

"As a matter of fact, I do. I invited an old friend, a rancher from near Tulsa. We haven't seen each other for years, so I'm looking forward to spending time with him. He isn't here yet, so you all go on down. Don't keep those cowboys waiting any longer."

Erin's knees shook, and she took a deep breath. Her first formal dance, and she would be going with Jake. She hoped it worked out. Over the past few days, they'd both been busy but seemed to have put their arguments behind them and agreed not to discuss any of their baggage at the dance. Maybe the evening would work out, after all.

Arm in arm, the three of them walked down the wide, curving staircase to the three men waiting for them at the bottom. "Don't they look handsome?" Hayley whispered.

"And all three in cowboy hats," Glory said with a quiet giggle. "I hope they shined their boots."

Erin couldn't remember seeing her brothers so spiffed up since Luke's senior prom, two years after the death of their parents. Tears stung her eyes, and she hoped no one noticed.

The moment she glanced at Jake, she knew she could be herself, and she offered him a smile.

The men all talked at once, but she only heard Jake. “I almost didn’t recognize you, until you smiled,” he said. “You look— I don’t know. *Beautiful* isn’t good enough.”

Her face heated with a blush, and he handed her a clear box that contained a corsage of deep pink roses and baby’s breath. She thanked him, and he helped her slip it on her wrist.

“I’d say your carriage awaits,” Jake said, “but we’re walking over to the Big Barn.”

The three couples walked together, eager to get to the party. The night was warm but not hot, with a slight breeze, and they talked and laughed, sharing memories of good times.

When they reached the barn, a line had formed at the door, and they waited for their turn to enter. Erin shivered at what the evening might bring, and Jake put his arm around her, pulling her close.

"Wait a minute," he said, holding her even closer. "Are you…"

Erin looked up at him. "Am I what?"

"You are. You're wearing perfume."

She sniffed, pretending to be insulted. "So?"

Leaning back, he took a long gaze at her from head to toe. "A dress *and* perfume?" He shook his head.

"Is there something wrong with that?" she said in her most indignant tone.

He made a strange face and nonchalantly said, "No. Nothing wrong."

Taking a step back, she glared at him. "Just because I wear jeans and cowboy boots most of the time doesn't mean I can't dress up."

"You're right," he said with a quick nod. "It doesn't."

"I don't know why you're so surprised. Women wear dresses and I'm a woman."

"You sure are."

The look in his eyes made her knees weak, while her heart did a flip-flop. "You noticed, huh?"

"About the time you hit twelve, sweetheart. And you've definitely grown since then." His gaze lingered on the low neckline of her dress.

She felt her face heat again and he pulled her closer.

"You bet I did. I just never expected you to become such a knockout."

Something in his eyes, his face, the way he looked at her, set off a fire in her. "I—" She took a deep breath and looked around. "The others have gone inside. Maybe we should, too."

But he didn't release her. "You think I'm kidding, don't you?"

Erin shrugged but wouldn't look at him. Nobody had ever said anything like that to her, and she didn't know what to think.

Lifting her chin with his finger, he forced her to look at him. "I don't say things I don't mean."

Completely undone, she took a step back to clear her head and felt alive again. "So, when you told me when I was seven that I was a frizzy-haired pain in the butt, you meant it?"

Jake tipped his head back and laughed. "As I recall, you'd just called me a toad-mouthed snake in the grass."

Her mouth flew open. "You remember that?"

The laughter in his eyes vanished. "I remember everything. *Everything.*"

Was that good or bad? Biting her bottom lip, she didn't know. But it was time to find out.

He slipped her hand through his arm and led her into the barn. Transformed with tiny white lights suspended from the two-story ceiling, the inside of the barn reminded her of a fairyland. Once her eyes adjusted to the dim lighting, she saw tables encircling a large dance floor, where a band was setting up on an elevated platform near one end.

"Do you see Dylan and Luke?" Jake asked.

She found them with Glory and Hayley at a table near a group of their friends. "There they are," she answered, pointing.

Feeling his arm go around her waist, she

looked up at the same time he looked down, and they shared a smile.

"What took you so long?" Luke asked when they reached the table.

Jake shrugged his broad shoulders as he pulled out a chair for Erin. "Some people like to take a leisurely stroll."

Luke's grin said he suspected something else. "Doesn't this place look great?" he said. "Glory, you did a bang-up job."

"I had a lot of help," Glory replied, smiling. "I told all my helpers how I wanted it to look, and they made it happen."

Now that she could see more clearly, Erin looked around the Big Barn. "What a big group we have," she said, waving to other friends nearby.

Feedback from the band's amplifiers ripped through the building, and they all covered their ears. "That's one way to get our attention," Dylan said.

The band kicked into a song, grabbing everyone's attention, and several couples walked onto the dance floor. Dusty stood and pulled at Kate's hand, but she shook her head. "Not yet," Erin heard her say. "Let's wait for something a little less noisy." But Dusty insisted.

"Want to join them?" Jake asked, as Erin tapped her foot to the country beat.

"Do you two-step?" she asked, scooting her chair back.

He stood and held out his hand to her. "Doesn't everybody?"

Laughing, she took his hand, and he led them to the dance floor, where they were surrounded by friends and neighbors. She'd never dreamed she would return home, much less to discover Jake back again, and in spite of what had happened, she felt a warm glow as he danced her around the floor. Tonight they would make new memories. If she did return to the circuit, at least she would have those.

JAKE NOTICED ERIN getting several admiring looks from both men and women and felt proud that she'd agreed to be his date. Their first. Officially, anyway.

They stayed on the floor for a second number, then by the third, the tempo slowed, and he took her in his arms. "Have I told you how beautiful you look tonight?" he asked, rubbing his thumb on her bare back. "And where'd you find this dress?"

She looked up at him, through long, darkened lashes. "Some store in Oklahoma City, where Glory took me. She wouldn't let me leave without buying it. I guess she was right."

"Oh, yeah, she was definitely right." He would have to remember to thank Glory.

"You know," Erin said, leaning closer, "Dusty reminds me of you, sometimes."

Jake didn't know if he should take that as a compliment or not. "Why's that?"

"He digs at Kate about as much as you dig at me." Grinning and wrinkling her nose at him, she turned her attention to the dancers.

"She seems to hold her own," he replied, watching the couple. "Just like you."

"And yet, just look at them," Erin said. "They adore each other."

"Yeah, they do," he said, holding her closer. He wanted to say that *he'd* always adored *her,* but the time wasn't right.

The song came to an end, and they returned to their table with Erin's brothers and their fiancées. Dylan collapsed in his chair. "I don't think I've had that much exercise since…I don't know. My baseball days, when Coach made us run laps, maybe?"

"You'd better start practicing," Glory told him. "We have our wedding dance in April. Hayley and I have booked this place for it and the reception."

"Already?" Luke asked.

Hayley nodded. "And after tonight, finding an open date will get even harder. Proms, birthdays, anniversaries, parties, you name it. I heard someone talking about having the Christmas bazaar here this year."

"All of those will pay for the renovations," Glory added. "Hettie gave me full rein, but it took a bank loan to do it."

"I didn't realize," Luke replied.

Erin leaned forward. "It's worth all the work you and the others put into it, Glory. It's perfect."

Jake leaned close and whispered in her ear. "And so are you." But he was a little envious, too. Except for Dylan and Glory, and Luke and Hayley, who still had to tie the knot, everyone else there had families. But at least he had Jonah. His son. And although he hadn't had the experience the others had of seeing his son born and watching him grow up, he counted himself lucky. He wanted to share the news with everyone, but he and Erin had agreed that they would wait until she had the chance to tell her brothers. After that, they would let the others know. Soon, he thought. Soon they might be that family he'd hoped for.

Beside him, Erin chatted with the other ladies about things completely foreign to him. Watching all the others, he realized how many good friends he'd made as a boy in Desperation. If that was all he had in the end—that and knowing Jonah—he wouldn't complain. But he wanted more. He wanted Erin. He knew that now.

Jake talked ranching with Luke and Dylan, while Erin talked babies and weddings with the other women. Toes tapped to the music, and laughter floated through the Big Barn. When the band announced their last set, the dance floor filled again.

"Thanks for a wonderful night, Jake," Erin said as he held her close. "Sometimes I get so busy with other things, I forget how special it is to spend time with friends."

"I think we're all that way," he answered. "They're the best. I'm glad I came back."

She tipped her head back and looked at him. "I am, too. It's times like this that I wonder how much I've missed."

"There's plenty of time to catch up." He felt her nod, but she didn't reply. "Plenty of things to do in Desperation, and we'll all be seeing each other often."

"We will," she said with a smile.

Before he knew it, the last song ended, and they gathered their things from the table, telling everyone goodbye and making plans to get together again soon.

"Do you want us to bring Jonah home when we get back?" Luke asked.

Jonah had offered to watch Brayden while the grown-ups attended the dance. "Whatever is easiest," Jake answered. "Have you heard anything from him?"

"Not a word," Hayley answered. "Brayden adores him, so I'm not surprised."

"They seemed to make a connection that night of the barbecue at your place," Jake said.

"Almost as if they were kin," Hayley said.

Jake nodded, trying hard not to look at Erin to see what her reaction might be. "He's a good kid. And he's learned a lot, thanks to Erin. I think you'll be surprised, Luke, at how good he is."

"He might as well spend the night," Luke answered. "He's going to help Dylan and me bring some of the cattle up tomorrow."

"That's what he said. Let me know how that goes."

"We will, but I don't expect any problems."

They reached the door and stepped outside into the warm, night air, where they waited long enough for Dylan and Glory to join them. Together, they walked to the Commune, where Glory and Erin went inside to get their things, before the drive home.

"Couldn't ask for a nicer night," Dylan said after the others were inside.

"A beauty," Jake agreed.

After a moment of silence, Dylan spoke again.

"Luke and I want you to know how nice it is to see you and Erin together again."

Jake's heart missed a beat, and he looked at him. "Again?"

Dylan grinned as a chuckle rumbled from his chest. "Yeah, we knew there was something going on between you two when we were kids. She took it hard when you left."

Nodding, Jake sighed, thinking of how he'd broken it off with her. "She wasn't the only one."

"I've always wondered about that."

Jake wasn't sure how to answer. Even Erin didn't know the whole story. Maybe someday he would tell her. Someday when they were old and gray with grandchildren. But there was plenty of time for that. Now that she'd come home, and they'd rediscovered what he thought they'd lost, there were things to catch up on.

"Let's just say it had to happen," he told Dylan. "I guess it wasn't the right time for us. She wanted—"

"To join the rodeo," Dylan finished. "And she did. We missed her bossy ways for a long time."

"Excuse me? Who's bossy?"

Both of them laughed and turned to see Erin coming down the long steps of the Commune.

"Nobody," Jake answered.

"As if I believe that," she said with a sniff.

When she reached them, Jake took the small bag she carried and grinned at her. "Believe what you want. You will anyway."

She made a face at him and started to answer, but Dylan cut her off. "There's Glory," he said as she joined them.

The four of them talked for a few minutes about what a good time they'd all had, then said their good-nights and went on to their trucks to start for home. To Jake's delight, Erin scooted over to sit next to him.

"It really was fun," she said, leaning her head on his shoulder.

He closed his eyes for a moment and enjoyed

having her next to him. "I hear they plan to do it every year."

"That would be nice."

The drive out of town didn't last long, and they were soon past the first two curves and nearing the Walker place. Erin straightened and covered a yawn with her hand.

"Tired?" he asked.

"A little, but it's a good tired."

"I know what you mean."

"I'm not ready to call it a night."

He glanced at her, wondering what she might be thinking. Easing his foot off the gas pedal, he answered her. "Me, either."

The smile she gave him was pure enchantment. "Your place or mine?" she asked.

He didn't need time to think about it. "Mine. There happens to be a bottle of champagne chilling in the refrigerator."

"Perfect."

Chapter Nine

"This really is a beautiful house," Erin said, taking in everything as Jake gave her a tour. "I don't recall ever being in it when we were growing up. Are these your uncle's furnishings?"

"Some," he said, "but I've made a few changes."

She didn't remember him being all that interested in things like colors and decorating. She hadn't been, either, and she wanted to learn how much he'd changed over the years they'd been apart. "Show me."

As they walked down a wide hallway, the heels of her fancy shoes clicking on the polished wood floor, he pointed out several paintings. "I picked these up at different places, here and there. Arizona, New Mexico, Nevada."

She studied the beautiful landscapes hanging on the walls, and turned to him. "You traveled around a lot?"

"A little. I worked at four different ranches over the past…well, I guess it's been about thirteen years. I learned something new at each one, so it was worth it." He walked farther down the hall and stopped before reaching a closed door. "Bedroom," he said, cocking his head toward it.

"Later," she answered. She nearly laughed as he tried to cover a smile, and then she turned back down the hall to where they'd started.

"Uncle Carl enjoyed luxury," he said, following her. "It's a good thing he was as successful as he was. Most people wouldn't build a house that's far too large for them, but I think he liked to show off."

In the kitchen, she stopped and leaned against the breakfast bar that separated the kitchen from the dining room. "Much different than the way I grew up."

He walked to the refrigerator and opened it. "But you had more fun than I did."

She smiled, remembering her childhood. "I did have fun. We all did. But we worked hard, too. You should remember that."

"I do." He closed the refrigerator and turned around, a bottle of uncorked champagne in his hand. "As promised," he said, and directed her to where the glasses were kept.

While she retrieved two slender champagne flutes, he popped the cork, with only a little bubbly overflow. "You've obviously done this before, Mr. Canfield."

"Once or twice." He led her back to the living room, where she put the glasses on a large low table.

He poured the champagne into the glasses, and she took the one he offered. After setting the bottle aside, he took her hand and settled her on the long red sofa, then sat next to her. "Comfortable?"

"It's about as perfect as it could get," she admitted. "Do we have a toast?"

His face went blank, and then he smiled. "We do. Or I do, I guess, now that you ask." He lifted his glass and she did the same. His eyes met hers, serious, but with a touch of wariness. "To new beginnings."

"And new memories," she added.

Instead of taking a drink, he leaned closer and kissed her, long, sweet and tender.

"And to us," he added, "if that's what you want."

Filled with feelings she'd forgotten, she managed a nod. She took a sip of the champagne and leaned against the back of the sofa.

"Whew," he breathed, tugging at his tie and the collar of his studded shirt with his free hand. "It's a little warm in here."

"Take off your jacket and tie," she said. "I don't mind."

The grin he shot her nearly made her toes curl. "Good idea."

Standing, he pulled off the jacket, jerked his fancy bowtie loose and undid the collar button, while she took a big drink from her glass.

Jacketless, the ends of his tie dangling on his shirtfront, he started to sit beside her again but stopped. "Want me to top that off?" he asked, indicating her glass with a nod.

"Yes, please," she answered with what she hoped was a seductive smile.

He took her glass, filled it to near the brim and settled next to her again. "Courage?" he asked her as she took another sip.

"Thirsty," she answered. Setting the glass out of the way, she leaned closer to kiss the corner of his upturned mouth. As she did, her fingers found the studs on his shirt, and she began to tug at them. When he put his hands over hers, she stopped and looked up at him.

"We're not doing this again," he said, his voice rough but quiet. "Not like before."

She shook her head and caught his gaze. “No, not like before.”

His struggle showed on his face. “Erin, I—”

“Hush,” she whispered, and took her time with the studs. Done, she set them aside and slowly spread his shirt open to place her hands on his chest. She felt his sharp intake of air and trailed the tips of her fingers down to the waistband of his tuxedo pants. Before she realized he’d moved, he had her beneath him, lying on the sofa. With one finger, he traced the low neckline of her dress.

“Are you trying to seduce me?” she asked.

“Turnabout’s fair play,” he whispered. His lips followed the path of his fingers, and her breathing quickened while the rest of her felt as if she’d fallen into a warm pool of water. Images of the one night they’d shared, years before, drifted through her mind. And she knew what she wanted to do.

“I have an idea,” she whispered.

“So do I,” he whispered back, nuzzling her ear.

"Let's go to the barn."

He stopped and raised his head to look at her. "Why?"

She saw the indecision in his eyes, but this was something she needed to do. "To make new memories."

"But you're in that dress and—"

"It's a dress, Jake, nothing more." Her thoughts came together quickly. "We can take a couple of blankets and pillows, the champagne, some—"

On his feet beside the sofa, he studied her. Looking more handsome than she ever remembered, he gazed straight into her eyes.

"I need this, Jake," she said, meaning it. Watching him, she waited, determined to win, whatever it took.

After a few seconds, he dropped his hands to his side. "If that's what you really want."

"It is."

"Then let me get something to carry some of these things in."

He left her on the sofa, and she finished off both her champagne and his. In only a few minutes, he returned with a large backpack and blankets. She watched as he stuffed the blankets, bottle and glasses into the bag.

When they were both ready, he held her hand and led her outside and across to the barn, but he stopped before they entered it. "You're sure about this?"

She'd never been more certain about anything. "Completely."

As they stepped into the pitch-black barn, he pulled a flashlight from his pocket, then grabbed a lantern from beside the door. "Let's hope the matches are here."

Before he could check, she felt on the bottom of the lantern and pulled off one of the matches taped to it. "This should work."

In the beam of the flashlight, she saw his grin. "You remember," he said as she lit the lantern. "There's another one in the loft. Stay down here until I light it," he ordered, and approached the ladder to the loft.

Knowing it wouldn't do any good to argue, she stood at the bottom of the ladder, ready to climb after him.

Erin waited until he made it to the top and saw the light from the second lantern. "Heads up," she called to him. He looked over the side of the loft, and she tossed him one of the pillows.

"You've got an arm like Dylan," he said, catching it and the second one she threw.

"We're a talented family," she answered as she kicked off her high heels. Pulling her dress up to her thighs, she began to climb. It took some doing, but she finally made it up far enough to see above the loft floor. Jake, standing over her, reached out his hand and helped her to the loft floor.

"What do you think?" he asked, leading her farther into the big loft.

She looked around and saw a cleanly swept

floor and a large mound of hay that had spilled from the many bales. "Better than I expected. Hand me the blankets and pillows."

Smiling, he shook his head and gave them to her. "Only you would want to do this."

While she spread the blankets on the hay, he pulled the champagne and glasses from the bag and put them on the floor. When she'd finished, she settled on them, plumping the pillows. "Come try it out."

He lowered himself next to her and glanced around. "You know, this idea of yours isn't half-bad."

As he spoke, she spread open his shirt and took up where she'd left off in the house.

"You're getting ahead of me," he whispered, then stood to pull her to her feet. "Now, this is some dress you have on, but I think we can do without it."

"Definitely." She nearly died as he took his time sliding it down and over her hips, painfully slow, to drop it to the floor. Heat curled through her as she stood in front of him in a black bustier and nearly-not-there panties.

"It just keeps getting better," he said, returning the two of them to the blanket and pillows. "But how do I get you out of it?"

She moved to give him her back. "Unhook it."

He didn't waste his time, and his fingertips burned their way down her back. With a deep moan, he leaned her back onto the pillows and captured her mouth with his. Closing her eyes as her hands explored him, she memorized the feel of this new and oh-so-grown-up Jake.

He left her for a few moments as he shed the rest of his clothes and added protection, then joined her again to stoke the blaze he'd set off in her, kissing all available spots…and more.

"I'm not going to try to talk you out of this, Erin," he said, his lips touching hers. "So if you plan to change your mind, now's the time."

Without answering, she wound her arms around his neck and kissed him deeply to let him know that there would be no turning back.

They touched and tasted every inch of each other until he entered her so slowly she wanted to beg him to hurry. How he knew every place to touch her, every move to take her closer to the edge, she didn't know, but somehow he did, then set the world spinning around her.

When the world righted again, she lay in his arms, her breathing and heart rate slowing to normal. Memories of the other time drifted into her mind, and she pushed them away.

She watched as he poured more champagne, and thought about the two things she wanted more than anything. The first was to return to the circuit and leave as a winner. Not the big time. Not Nationals. That didn't matter as much now. But a winner, nonetheless.

Now that she didn't have a secret to keep from him, they might have a chance. But he'd never told her he loved her. Did he? She thought he did, but she needed to hear him say it. She knew it was crazy, but three little words would make the difference.

JAKE STEPPED OUT of Erin's RV and blinked at the bright sunshine that hit him in the face like a sledgehammer. At some point during the night, he'd walked her home. Driving might have been easier, but considering how late it had been, he'd been afraid the sound of a vehicle in the middle of the night might alert Dylan. While he now knew both Dylan and Luke were pleased that he and Erin were getting along, he couldn't be sure how they might react if they learned he and their sister had spent the night together. The whole night. He'd planned to go back home, but one thing led to another and then another—the barn, her RV—and they'd both fallen asleep. Now all he had to do was get away without—

"Hey, Jake!"

Damn. So much for not being seen. At least he'd been smart enough to insist he and Erin change out of their fancy duds before he'd walked her home.

Shading his eyes with his hand, he saw Jonah walking toward him. "Hey, Jonah. I thought you were helping Dylan and Luke today."

"I am," the boy answered, "but Dylan sent me to make sure Erin had survived the party last night."

"Same reason I'm here," Jake said. "She's good." An understatement, for sure.

"Want to come with us to round up the next bunch?"

Knowing he shouldn't stay around much longer, Jake declined the invitation. "I'll pass. I need to get back and check on Bella. She's about to foal any day."

"I'd sure like to be there when that happens."

Jake put a hand on his shoulder. "You can count on it."

Behind him, the door opened, and he started to say something to warn Erin, but he wasn't quick enough.

"Jake," she said, her voice a purr. "Why don't you—" Her hair a jumble of curls, she stared, openmouthed at Jonah. “Oh! Hi, Jonah. I thought I heard voices and—”

“He stopped by to see how the party went last night,” Jake said in a rush.

Jonah, eyes wide, staring at her, nodded.

She ran her fingers through her hair as if that would tame it. “We had lots of fun,” she said.

“Right,” Jake agreed. “Good music, good company. An all-around good time for everybody.”

“That’s what Dylan and Luke said.” Jonah looked at Erin, who didn’t seem at all comfortable with the situation. “We’re getting ready to head out to round up another bunch of cattle. Want to come with us?”

She gave Jake a quick, puzzled look before answering. “I have a dozen things to do today. Laundry, dishes. You know. I’ll have to pass, but maybe next time.” She looked up, past them, and Jake heard her sigh. “There’s Dylan,” she said. “It must be time to get those cattle.”

No one spoke again until Dylan reached

them. “I see you both survived the dance,” he told Erin and Jake.

“Survived and looking forward to another one next year,” Jake answered with sincerity. By then, he hoped his and Erin’s relationship had taken the turn he hoped for. They still had a few things to work through.

Dylan’s eyes narrowed as he looked at his sister. “Did you just crawl out of bed?”

She shook her head. “Oh, no. I’ve been up for a while. Just lazing around. After all, it’s Sunday.”

“The cattle don’t know that,” he replied. “I take it you’re not going to ride along with us?”

She shook her head. “I have women’s work to do.”

“Right,” he said, and turned to Jake. “How about you?”

Glad that he already had an excuse, Jake shook his head. “Jonah already asked, but I have a mare about to foal, so I’ll have to say no.”

"Too bad. You'd enjoy it. Jonah's proved to be quite a cowboy, thanks to you and Erin."

"Erin gets the thanks," Jake said, and smiled at her. "She trained him. I couldn't be more proud of both of them."

Jonah beamed with what could only be pride but said nothing.

"Well," Dylan said, "we'd better get to work, Jonah. With three of us, it shouldn't take long. I'll take you back to Jake's when we're done. Say, around five or so?"

"Sounds good," Jake answered, relieved they were leaving.

Erin opened the door a little wider but didn't step out. "Did you want to come in, Jake?" she asked.

He nearly swallowed his tongue and hoped Jonah didn't catch on that he'd said he'd checked on her. Watching Dylan and Jonah walk away, while trying to decide what to do, he saw Dylan look back and smile. "Sure," Jake said. "For a minute."

He'd barely stepped inside, when she pushed the door shut. "What the hell is going on?" she demanded.

Jake shrugged. "Jonah walked up just as I came out the door. I did the best I could do, considering. And then you invited me in again."

"Great," she said, starting to pace the room. "Just great." She stopped and looked at him. "Do you think he suspected anything?"

He ran his hand through his hair and discovered a piece of hay. "Beats me."

"We'll have to be more careful."

"Not an easy thing to do, what with you living here, where Dylan can see all the going in and out, and Jonah at my place in the bunkhouse."

Worrying her lip, she nodded. "We'll have to think of something."

"Dylan already suspects there's something going on."

Her head came up and she stared at him. "And why do you think that?"

"He said something last night after the dance

about how happy he and Luke are to see that we're getting along so well." But her concern bothered him. "Does it really matter that much?"

"Maybe," she answered, gripping her hands in front of her. "It depends." She shook her head. "I don't know. There are so many things they don't know, and I—"

"Erin," he said, taking her hands in his. He led her to the small sofa and settled her on it, then sat beside her. "We need to give some thought to telling them who Jonah is. They have a right to know he's their nephew."

"I know," she said. "But I don't know how to tell them." She raised her head to look at him. "I don't want it to cause any trouble between you and them."

"There's always that chance," he admitted. "But I kind of doubt they can claim, um, purity themselves, if you get my meaning." Her weak laughter gave him hope. "We'll tell them together."

"No," she answered. "I'll do it myself. I'm the one who kept the secret. You didn't know."

"That still doesn't exonerate me from—"

"What big words you use, Jake," she said, smiling at him. "But it's still my responsibility. And it will give them time to cool down, if needed."

He understood. He hadn't taken the news easily, either. "Okay, but if you change your mind—"

Her curls bounced when she shook her head. "I won't. But I'll have to pick the right time."

"Soon," he said. "As soon as possible. If they learn from Jonah, they won't be happy."

Her eyes widened. "You don't think Jonah would tell them, do you?"

"No. Not right away." At least he hoped not. Hearing it from Jonah would make matters worse. He knew that from experience. "I think Jonah understands that it wouldn't be his place to be the one to tell them."

"You're right," she said. "I'll do it as soon as I

can get them together. I don't want to do it more than once. Although," she added, "the thought of them ganging up on me isn't pleasant." As if she knew what he was thinking, she smiled. "Don't try to play white knight. I can handle it *and* come out the winner."

"We're both winners." He leaned closer and kissed her but forced himself to keep it short, then got to his feet. "I'd better get home."

"I wish you didn't have to," she said, standing. "And it's a good thing I pulled on this robe before I opened the door."

"Why's that?"

"Because they might have been surprised at what I'm wearing under it." She untied her robe and opened it.

He groaned at the sight of her very naked body. "Yeah," he managed to say, "they surely would have." Without thinking he reached out to touch her, but she quickly closed her robe and tied it.

"Later," she said with a wicked smile.

He reined in his hormones and tried to frown. “You are one evil woman, Erin Walker.”

She didn’t say a word as he turned for the door, opened it and checked to make sure no one was around before he stepped outside. If he’d thought the day was hot earlier, it was blistering now. “See you *later,*” he said, looking back at her, standing in the doorway.

She smiled again and wiggled her fingers in a goodbye wave before she shut the door. He blew out a breath, glad to have the walk home to cool down.

FRESHLY SHOWERED AT Dylan’s house, Erin dressed quickly. If her RV had been connected to the waterline, she wouldn’t have had to make the trip to the house each day for a shower. Most days, Dylan spent his spare time with Glory, often at Luke’s house. Knowing he would be busy for a while with Luke and Jonah, she’d hurried over as soon as Jake had gone home.

Even knowing she would soon have to tell

her brothers about Jonah, she smiled at herself in the mirror as she combed through her wet, tangled hair. Jake had helped her banish the bad memories of the night Jonah had been conceived, and she would never have to deal with them again.

If only...

But she shook the thought away. She couldn't turn back time and wouldn't, even if given the chance. At least she'd been given the gift of meeting and knowing the son she'd never thought to see again.

And then there was Jake.

Sighing at the happiness that surged through her, in spite of no declaration of love from him, she grabbed her things and headed downstairs. Before she reached the bottom, she heard the kitchen door shut and wished she didn't have to face her brother. She would have to pretend and skirt around any questions he might have, until the time came to share her story with him and Luke.

"Erin?" he called out. "Are you here?"

"Yes, it's me. I needed a shower after that party last night."

"That was some shindig," he said when she walked into the kitchen. "I've never been one for dances. Never liked them. But I have to admit last night might have changed my mind."

She had to grin. Dylan had crawled into himself after their parents died, and she'd worried about him for years. Directing Glory to him had made the difference. The change had come slowly, but she felt aglow each time she saw that he'd returned to the Dylan she remembered before the accident.

"It was fun," she said, "and I'm glad you went."

"I'm glad we all went."

"Are you finished with the cattle today?"

He nodded. "It didn't take near as much time as I'd expected. I meant it when I said Jonah is good. But then you were the one who taught him, so I shouldn't be surprised."

She felt the warmth of his praise spread

through her. "He's a good kid. Eager to learn and quick."

"Yeah, he is. I hope Jake will let us borrow him again sometime. But he said he'd be leaving next month."

"School," she said quickly.

"Yeah, that's what he said," Dylan answered, "but he didn't seem to want to talk about it."

It wasn't the right time to explain. "He doesn't talk about it much. And I need to get back to my place. Is Glory coming by later?"

"She is. Luke and Hayley are coming over with Brayden. Jonah said he might stop by, too. He sure does like that little guy."

Easing toward the door and hoping to slip out soon, she said. "Brayden's easy to like."

Dylan grinned. "That he is."

"You and Glory will have your own before long."

"We hope to."

"Then I'll let you get cleaned up," she said,

stepping out onto the porch. “I’ll see you in the morning.”

“Erin,” he said, stopping her.

Wishing he’d let her be on her way, she turned to him.

“Be good to Jake,” he said. “He’s a good guy. One of the best.”

Not knowing how to answer, she nodded and hurried outside and on her way home. What would Dylan say— Luke, too—when they learned what had happened almost eighteen years ago? She didn’t want to think about it, so she didn’t, and by the time she reached her motor home, she’d managed to turn her thoughts in another direction.

Jake’s mare would soon foal, and she wanted to be there. So did Jonah, and she hoped Jake would allow it. She couldn’t think of a reason he might not, but she would be prepared with all the arguments needed, if he did.

Smiling, she opened her door to the sound of her phone. She’d forgotten and left it behind when she went to Dylan's, and she had to scramble to find it before the caller gave up.

"Hello?" she said.

"Erin! Erin Walker!"

Erin smiled at the familiar voice. "Shelly Roberts! I haven't heard from you for months."

"I know," Shelly answered. "I've been busy. But I miss racing against you."

Settling back on the sofa, Erin laughed but felt a pang of envy. "I wasn't that much competition before I left."

"That wasn't your fault," her friend said. "Training a new horse isn't easy. How's that going?"

"Good," Erin said with a smile. "I've finally got a handle on it, and so does he." Thanks to Jake pointing out that it might be her problem, not MacDuff's, her training had paid off, and her horse was ready to compete.

"Then you're ready to come back?"

"I plan to," Erin answered honestly. She simply hadn't decided when and where, but it hadn't exactly been her top priority for the past few days.

"Great! Because the Chandler Open starts Friday."

Erin's heart leaped at the news. To compete again had been her goal since leaving the circuit behind. And now she had the opportunity. Should she take it? It would mean leaving Jonah and Jake, at least for a short time. Only days, really. Unless...unless she could win a purse big enough for the entry fee for another.

Torn between missing them and the chance to compete again, she couldn't decide. "That soon? I don't know," she answered.

"Oh, please, Erin," Shelly said. "I know it's short notice, but you can do it. It's hardly an hour drive. And, yeah, it's a smaller rodeo compared to others, but it's the perfect place for a comeback."

She had a point. "As long as I win or at least place," Erin said.

"You will," Shelly assured her. "You're that good, no matter what horse you're riding."

Laughing, Erin shook her head. "Against you? That definitely means a win or place isn't a given."

"Well, that's the thing," Shelly said, with a soft laugh. "I won't be competing."

"What?" Erin could hardly believe what she heard. "Why not?"

"Steve put his foot down."

"I can't believe he'd do that," Erin said. "Being a bronc rider, he knows what it is to have rodeo in your blood."

"He does, but he wants me to take it easy. I'm about halfway through this pregnancy, and believe me, this second one is going to be an elephant. I'm so big already that I feel like a beached whale."

"Pregnant? Oh, Shelly, that's wonderful!" Erin cried. "How does Grayson feel about having a little brother or sister?"

"Excited. Most of the time," Shelly added

with a chuckle. “But he’s old enough now that he doesn’t have to be watched every second. My sister has promised to help when the baby gets here and I start riding again.”

Erin wished she could tell her friend her own news, that she, too, had a son. But her brothers deserved to know before anyone else. “How perfect for you. Steve, too. How’s he doing?”

“Good,” Shelly replied. “He’s cut back a little to spend more time with me, but he’s been doing well.” She hesitated for a moment, leaving a silence between them. “So well, in fact, that your entry is already paid. So, see, you have to go to Chandler.”

“You didn’t!” Erin said with a groan. “Shelly, you shouldn’t have done that.”

“I knew it would be the only way to get you there,” Shelly said. “Besides, we had the extra. We decided if I can’t compete right now, then you should. Can’t let those young girls get ahead of us.”

Erin felt tears coming on and took a deep

breath, hoping to stop them. She and Shelly had been friends for many years. They'd competed against each other, both winning and losing, and they'd been each other's fan club. But to pay her entry fee? Erin couldn't imagine. And she couldn't take it.

"Shelly, I can't let you do that."

"Too late. It's a done deal."

Erin knew there were times when entry fees could be given to someone else. "What about a trade policy?"

"Not at this rodeo."

Quickly calculating the cost and knowing she had the travel money, Erin still didn't have an answer. "Can I let you know?"

"Sure," Shelly said.

Erin felt awful that she might let her friend down, but she couldn't give her a definite answer. She only had one option. "I'll pay you back, Shelly. I don't know if I can make it to Chandler, but I'll pay you back for the entry fee, no matter what."

"You don't have to do that, hon," Shelly replied. "It isn't a lot, and we want to do this for you. Steve and I both do. I know you left because money ran out. With Firewind gone and the trouble you had with your new horse, well, it happens. It could happen to me one day, too."

"No, it won't," Erin told her. "You'll stop before that happens, regroup and be back riding again. I should have stopped sooner instead of thinking it would get better. And it's been nice to be home again."

"I'm glad," Shelly said, her voice sincere. "I know you avoided it, although you never said why."

Erin smiled. "It's nothing I can talk about yet, but someday soon I'll tell you about it."

"That sounds very intriguing," Shelly teased. "When you're ready to talk, let me know."

"I will," Erin promised. "And I'll call you in a few days and let you know if I'll be riding in Chandler."

"Fair enough. By Thursday, if you can. We want to be there to watch you."

"And cheer me on, I hope," Erin replied, laughing. "Thank you, Shelly. I never expected—"

"Of course you didn't. That's what makes this so much fun."

After they ended the conversation, Erin sat on the sofa with the phone in her hand and her thoughts on what she could do. She hadn't expected any of this. Not seeing Jake again or realizing how much she still cared for him, in spite of the way he'd left her. Or meeting Jonah, only to learn he was their son. And the night before, after the dance. How could she simply walk out?

The pain of the words he'd said to her the night before he returned to college still lingered. It didn't take much to remember how cold and emotionless he had been after they'd made love that first night and how her heart had never completely healed from it. Even now.

She didn't know if what she had now or might

have in the future would be enough to keep her from her life's dream. She wanted to be a winner again. She knew she could do it, but she wanted to prove to everyone else that she could.

But could love be the one thing she needed more? She'd never loved anyone except Jake. But she didn't know for certain that he loved her the way she needed him to. If she stayed, would it last? Would he still be there if she left? She didn't have an answer.

Chapter Ten

"Hey, boss."

Finishing the last of his instructions to Bobby Ray, Jake turned around. "What is it, Kelly?"

Kelly didn't speak until he was within a few feet from Jake. "Well, I found something in the barn."

Jake glanced down to see an object in Kelly's hand. Something dark. Something he'd seen only a few days before. Something with a tall heel. Erin's shoe.

"There's another one in the barn just like it," Kelly explained, "but I thought I'd look a little funny if I carried both of them out here. You know? With all the others watching?"

Biting the inside of his cheek to keep from smiling, Jake looked around the ranch yard and saw that no one had noticed Kelly or what he had. He held out his hand. "Strange place to find a pair of ladies' high-heeled shoes, huh?"

Kelly handed the shoe over to him. "First thing I thought was that they belonged to Miss Erin, but I don't think she's the kind who'd wear something like them."

Jake nearly choked. Kelly would be surprised to discover what Miss Erin would wear…or not wear. "Probably some high school kids, necking in the barn," he managed to say with a straight face.

"That's what I thought, too." Without another word, Kelly turned and walked away, headed back to the barn.

Shoe in hand, Jake started for the house, with the hope that no one would notice what he had. He made it to the door but heard footsteps coming up the steps behind him. Looking over his shoulder, he saw Gary behind him on the porch, wearing a grin.

"I never would have guessed your feet were so small," Gary said.

Too late to hide the shoe, Jake frowned. "Kelly found it in the barn. I guess some teenagers were having a good time in there, while I was in town."

"Reasonable enough, I guess. However…"

"However what?"

"I would've thought you'd have noticed if anybody came around, but I heard you accompanied the lovely Miss Walker to some big dance on Saturday night."

Jake tried to play it cool and squinted into the bright morning sunlight. "Did you, now?"

"I guess those teenagers took advantage of the place while you were gone," Gary said, as polite as could be. "I'd lay odds that you had a better evening than they did. You know, with all that hay and all."

"You're about to step over the line, my friend," Jake replied in warning.

Gary, his expression serious, tipped his hat back with a thumb. "I really like Erin," he said, keeping eye contact with Jake. "We all do. What we wouldn't like is for her to get hurt."

"I can assure you that isn't going to happen."

Gary slapped him on the shoulder. "I didn't think so but wanted you to know how we all feel about our lady wrangler. She's a good one. Don't screw it up."

With no way to answer, Jake nodded and watched Gary start down the porch steps. They'd been good friends for several years. He needed to ease up on him. After all, every one of the men had taken to Erin and treated her with respect. But then she'd earned it. She worked as hard as they did and as long. Many men might have resented that. Not his crew.

"Gary," he called out. When Gary looked over his shoulder, Jake waved him back to the porch. When Gary joined him, he kept his voice low. "Just so you know, I appreciate that you're looking out for her. Don't let her know you're doing it, though. If she thinks you're playing big brother, she'll rip you up one side and down the other." He smiled, having had that honor, more than once. "I can tell you from personal experience, it won't be pleasant."

Gary nodded and chuckled but was cut short by Jonah, who appeared with an announcement. "It's time, Jake."

Gary slapped Jake on the back. "Let us know how Bella does. I've never seen anybody so wrapped up in the birth of a foal as Erin is."

"She's been in that barn since just after midnight," Jake said. "We put in a cot for her, but she hasn't done anything but sit on it. No nap, no nothing." He turned to Jonah. "Tell her I'll be right there with the hot water and towels and cigars."

Gary laughed, but Jonah studied him for a moment. "You really want me to tell her that?"

Chuckling, Jake shook his head. "No, just that I'm on my way. We have a little time."

A few minutes later, he found Erin and Jonah in the foaling shed that had been completed only days before he'd offered her a job. Sitting on an old, three-legged milking stool in the nearly spotless stall, she didn't seem to know anyone had entered.

"Can't you find something more comfortable?" he asked her. "You know this could take a little time."

She raised her face to his, worry in her eyes. "Does that mean this is a good time to take a coffee break?"

He was far more concerned about her than the mare. "If that's what you want to do, but you know I'll bring you anything you want."

"Then bring me a little filly, safe and sound and healthy."

Checking to make sure no one other than Jonah had come into the barn, he hunkered down next to her and put his arm around her. "Bella's healthy, and her foal will be, too."

Nodding, she turned her attention back to the mare. "I know, but I worry all the same."

"Well, don't. And don't get mad if it isn't a filly."

She turned to him with a smile. "I won't. I promise."

"How long?" Jonah asked.

"Could be a few minutes," Jake answered.

"Could be an hour," Erin said at the same time. When she laughed, Jake felt better.

Fifteen minutes passed as Bella lay on the floor of the stall. "It won't be long now," Erin said, on her knees next to the mare's head, stroking her neck.

Looking a little pale, Jonah asked, "What's that?"

Erin moved to see. "The hoof! We're almost there."

"That's good," Jonah replied.

Jake reached for the wooden stool. "Sit down, Jonah, and enjoy the miracle."

Nodding, Jonah lowered himself to the stool but didn't take his eyes off the horse.

"Second hoof, and there's the nose," Erin announced.

"It can't breathe," Jonah cried out. "Do something."

"No need," Erin said, her voice calm. "The foal doesn't breathe until the shoulders are through. Now comes the hard part."

"Huh?" Jonah asked, white-faced and round-eyed.

"Watch or you'll miss it."

The mare bore down, and the foal's shoulders passed out, followed by the rest of it. "Wow," Jonah whispered.

Relieved of her baby, Bella stood on all four legs, and Jake turned to Jonah. "If you can tear yourself away, would you go tell Kelly that we're ready?"

Jonah stood, his legs obviously a little weak. "Why Kelly?"

"Beth, our veterinarian, has been schooling him on the next steps to be taken," Erin explained. "I think he's hoping Jake will start raising his own horses."

When Jonah had gone, Jake turned to Erin, who stood watching the colt struggle to stand. "Are you disappointed?"

She shook her head and laughed softly, her eyes sparkling. "Not at all. He's a beauty. Who could ask for more?"

"You have a name for him, I'm sure."

"As a matter of fact, I do."

"And?"

"Well, Bella is the name of a character in a book, and I thought about that, so I've decided on Twilight."

"*You* decided?" Jake asked, reaching out to pull her closer.

She nodded, grinning. "Unless, of course, you have something better?"

"Nope," he said. "It sounds perfect to me." Even knowing they could be interrupted at any moment, he kissed her, keeping it as brief as he could. No sense giving the help more reason to gossip.

When he released her, she stepped away. "If you'll keep an eye on them, I'll go call Beth with the news. She wanted us to let her know."

"I'll keep an eye out for Kelly," Jake said. As she started to step around him, he stopped her. "I'm glad you're happy."

She tipped her face up to his. "Why wouldn't I be?"

"No reason," he answered. But he saw something in her eyes that bothered him. She was obviously tired. He was, too, but happy. Since the day he'd discovered her lying in the grass at the pond, he'd been happier than he ever remembered being.

The sound of the heavy door being opened had them jumping apart, and she greeted Kelly and Jonah on her way out.

"Beautiful," Kelly said, stepping into the stall.

"Yeah," Jake answered, but he was thinking of Erin.

"HAVE YOU SEEN JAKE?" Erin asked Jonah.

Headed in the direction of the bunkhouse, he stopped. "Is something wrong?"

"No, nothing," she answered. Feeling a bit paranoid that somehow her conversation with Shelly had become known, she asked, "Why would you think that?"

"I don't know," he said with a shrug. "Just...I don't know. Try the barn. He may be in there."

"Thanks," she said, and turned around to go back that way. But she worried that Jonah had sensed something wasn't right. If he did, Jake might have, too, and she didn't want that to happen. She still hadn't made a decision and didn't see any reason why he should know about it until she knew what she wanted to do and felt ready to tell him.

She reached the barn and stepped inside but didn't see Jake, so she called his name.

"Back here, Erin. In the tack room," he answered from the far end of the barn.

Her boot heels tapped on the wooden walkway. The lonely sound didn't make her feel any more confident about what she would soon be doing. The scent of hay and horses enveloped her, reminding her that both were solid staples of her life, in many ways.

When she reached the end, she stepped inside the small room, where she saw piles of leather on the floor. "What in the world are you doing?" she asked.

Seated on a wooden bench, he tossed an old and very worn halter onto one of the piles. "I'm sorting all this to make more room. I thought Kelly had done it, but he'd only straightened up the place. There are things in here that are practically useless, and there's no reason to keep them around. If we need more, I'll buy more."

She noticed his use of *we* and wondered if he

meant the ranch or the two of them. But she didn't ask. Instead, she said, "Spoken like a successful rancher."

"That sounds good," he said with a grin, then returned to the jumble of leather in front of him. "Want to help?"

Hesitating at the thought of what she had to say, she forced herself to answer. "I would, but…"

His hands stilled and he looked up at her. "But what?"

She pulled in a deep breath. "I thought I should let you know that I'm going to Dylan's. Luke will be there soon, and—"

"You're going to tell them about Jonah," he finished for her.

He put the piece of leather aside and moved to stand, but she didn't want him to. If he touched her, kissed her, she'd lose her determination to get this thing done, and that wasn't like her. Once she made up her mind to do something—

"No, sit down," she told him.

"Are you okay?"

"Yes," she said, and sighed. "And no, but it's all right. I can't put it off any longer."

He nodded, his face serious and his eyes worried. "My offer to go with you still stands."

"I have to do it without you. I hope you understand that, Jake. I really do."

Closing his eyes, he shook his head. "I don't understand, but I won't insist."

When he opened his eyes, she saw the love she'd always wanted, but he still hadn't said it. Not in so many words. The one thing she needed desperately, especially now, he hadn't given her.

"Thank you, Jake," she said. "That means a lot to me."

"Erin," he said as she started for the door. She stopped and turned to look at him. "Let me know how it goes."

Trying for a smile, she answered, "I will."

In her home-on-wheels, she splashed her face with water from her portable water supply, checked herself in the mirror and decided she looked like a man on death row walking to the gallows. Not that there were any gallows left, but she had an idea how it must feel.

Her walk to Dylan's house was filled with if-onlys and what-ifs, and she reached her destination sooner than she'd hoped she would. Inhaling deeply and with a smile at the ready, she walked into the kitchen.

"Hey, Erin," Luke greeted her from his usual place at the table.

Dylan, across from him, pushed a chair back with his foot. "Have a seat, big sister."

She held back a laugh. He rarely admitted her seniority. "Thanks," she said, "but I'll stand, if that's all right."

"Suit yourself," he said with a shrug.

"Want a beer?" Luke asked, lifting the bottle on the table in front of him.

She made a face. "I never liked the taste of it. But…"

"But what?" Dylan asked.

She debated whether to ask or not, but decided it couldn't hurt. "Can either of you make a screwdriver?"

Luke glanced at Dylan before getting to his feet. "Easy as pie," he said.

"How's that new colt?" Dylan asked while Luke fixed her drink.

Glad to be able to talk about everyday things, she smiled and leaned back against the edge of the counter behind her. "He's a beauty. You need to go see him."

"Jonah said you named him Twilight."

She nodded, thinking of the beautiful addition to Jake's ranch. "It fits. You'll understand when you see him."

Luke handed her the filled glass. "We'll try to do that tomorrow."

She picked up the glass and took a long drink, then set it down. "Good grief, Erin," Dylan said.

"Thirsty," she said.

Her brothers glanced at each other, and Luke shrugged. "She's a big girl."

Gathering her courage and hoping her brothers would control their tempers—although she knew if she were in their shoes, she wouldn't be able to—she started with a question. "You both like Jonah a lot, don't you?"

"Sure," Luke answered first. "You've done some amazing things with him, Erin. It's like he was born to ride a horse and rope cattle."

"I'm really proud of him," she answered. "It's been an honor to teach him. He listens to everything and then does it. Not always perfect the first time, but quicker than most." She realized she'd said it too fast, and reached for her glass again.

"He's good with Brayden, too," Dylan said, glancing at Luke.

"Hayley thinks he's the best thing since sliced bread," Luke added.

Dylan leaned back in his chair, and she caught him watching her closely. "He's a natural," he said.

She took a sip of her drink and wrapped her

hands around the cold glass. "He should be," she said, and took another deep breath. "He's my son."

"Sure he is," Dylan said.

She looked from one brother to the other. "No, he's really my son. Mine and Jake's."

"We already had that figured out," Luke said.

Ready to argue, she realized what they'd said, but had trouble getting the words out. "You knew?"

"It's so obvious," Luke said, and winked at Dylan. "You'd think we were blind or something."

"But—"

"He has your talent, Erin," Luke continued.

"And Jake's smile."

"And your hair," Luke added. "Not quite so curly, though."

Dylan leaned forward and folded his arms on the table. "And he asks a zillion questions about both of you. And about Pop and Mama. Those were the clinchers."

She couldn't believe it. Too easy, she thought. Jonah must have— "Did he tell you?"

Dylan shook his head. "Not a word. Just a lot of questions."

"But by then," Luke said, "we'd pretty much figured it out."

Her legs nearly failed her, but she made it to the chair Dylan had offered earlier and sat on it. "How long have you known?"

"Not long," Luke said, "but we started putting two and two together. Or one and one, is more like it," he said with a grin. "We always wondered about that trip you took to Aunt Janelle's that summer. That woman hasn't been sick a day in her life. And she's still going strong."

Dylan continued. "Then when Jonah mentioned he lived in Kansas, we had a good idea what that trip had been about."

"You'd gained some weight, too," Luke said. "I don't think anybody else noticed, but we lived with you. We got to calling you Chunky Monkey behind your back."

She gasped. "You didn't!"

Both of them laughed, and Dylan got to his feet and moved to lean down and put his arm around her. "It couldn't have been easy for you. But it was easy for us, once we started putting the pieces of the puzzle together."

Luke stood and joined them. "Like those weeks after Jake came back for Thanksgiving but didn't stay. You spent a lot of time in the bathroom every morning."

Erin closed her eyes, thinking of how much her heart had hurt and the nights she'd cried herself to sleep, something she never did before. And the morning sickness she'd endured. "I didn't know until Jonah told us last week."

"You didn't guess he was your son?" Luke asked.

She shook her head, tears burning her eyes, but then she laughed. "And all this time I've been worried what you'd do when I told you."

"We're family, Erin," Luke said, giving her a brotherly hug. "We're here for each other, good or bad, right or wrong. And we don't judge each other or tell each other what to do." A chuckle escaped. "Okay, Dylan and I don't, but you sure messed around in our lives last year."

"And look what you gained," she pointed out. "Two beautiful brides-to-be."

They both kissed her cheeks, Luke on one side, Dylan on the other, and she felt her face burn with embarrassment and love.

After returning to their seats, Dylan tipped his chair back. "Jake seemed pretty happy this past week. Any plans yet?"

The question brought her back to earth and the question she hadn't yet answered for herself. "No, no plans."

Dylan looked at Luke. "Maybe it's time we have a talk with him."

"Couldn't hurt," Luke replied.

"No!" she cried. "Let it happen if it's supposed to."

"Supposed to?" Dylan asked. "And why the hell shouldn't it? Jake has always been crazy about you. And something tells me you feel the same. So isn't the next step making it permanent?"

Staring at her hands clasped on the table, she shook her head. "If it happens, let it. If it doesn't, then I'll—"

"You'll what?" Dylan asked.

She felt his gaze on her. "Whatever I decide."

"Not the rodeo circuit," Luke said.

Unwilling to tell them what had been on her mind after Shelly's call or the plans she'd had when she came home, she shrugged. "I never said that. Don't jump to conclusions that may not be true."

Luke blew out a breath. "Good, because we don't want you to leave."

"Family should be together," Dylan said.

"Of course," she answered, and hoped that would be the end of it. But she'd spent most of her life in rodeo, and she didn't know if she was ready to give it up completely. "And on that note," she said, "I need to get home. Another day, another dollar."

She pushed her chair back and stood, and so did her brothers. They talked for a few more moments, teasing and calling her Chunky Monkey, and she finally told them goodbye, laughing as she walked out the door. But the closer she got to her motor home, the less sure she felt she wouldn't be leaving.

Minutes later, inside her own little home, she knew she couldn't go see Jake and tell him what had happened. He would know immediately that something was bothering her. Instead, she reached for her phone and called him.

"Hey, Jake," she said when he answered. "You're going to love this."

"What's that?" he asked.

"Dylan and Luke already had it figured out."

"That Jonah is our son?" he asked carefully.

"Yes."

She heard silence for several seconds, and

then he started laughing. "Damn those brothers of yours," he said. "You're right, I do love it."

She wished he'd added that he loved her, but he didn't. And she knew what she had to do. She couldn't stay. She would find a way to see Jonah as often as she could, and she would stop at home, now and then. But if Jake couldn't tell her he loved her, she needed to move on.

"—surprised they haven't tarred and feathered me," Jake was saying.

"They wouldn't do that," she answered. They were family. Family loved each other, through good times and bad.

The reality of her decision hit her. What goes around, comes around, she thought. Jake had walked out on her, and now she would walk out on him.

JAKE WIPED THE sweat from his neck and glared at the sun. He knew from past experience that late July could be hotter than the hinges of hell, but that didn't mean he had to like it.

Midweek and over halfway into summer, he couldn't wait for the weekend. He had plans, plans that were even hotter than the day they were enduring. Even better, he had some things to say to Erin. All he could do was hope it turned out the way he wanted it to. If so, that family he'd dreamed of, that life of ranching with her by his side, would come true.

But he hadn't seen much of Erin all morning. The horses she and Jonah usually rode were gone, so he suspected she'd taken him for more lessons. Jake couldn't believe how well and quickly his son picked up on things. *His son.* He still hadn't adjusted to it and worried about the day, only a few weeks away, when Jonah would leave to go home. He knew it had to happen, but he didn't look forward to it.

Instead of letting it gnaw at him, he started adding to his plan. Maybe a dip in Lake Walker? A night under the stars? Something special, for sure. He'd even made a trip to Oklahoma City for the one thing he needed to tie up everything.

He saw Gary leave the barn and hailed him. "Have you seen Erin and Jonah?"

Crossing the wide ranch yard, Gary stopped in front of him. "Not since earlier this morning. I noticed Erin seemed a bit preoccupied with something."

Jake had noticed it, too. In fact, he'd thought it odd that she'd called him the evening before to let him know she'd told her brothers, when she could have told him in person. But at least that problem had been solved. He still had trouble believing they'd guessed, but he couldn't have been happier that they'd accepted it so easily.

Miracles happened, and the past few weeks had proven it. Now for just one more.

"Do you want me to go looking for them?" Gary asked.

Jake shook his head. "No need. They'll be back soon. Ada mentioned dinner is almost ready, and if Jonah can't smell it from wherever they are, Erin will."

Gary laughed and put his hand on Jake's

shoulder. "Ada's a treasure, that's for sure. Where did you find her?"

"Erin," Jake answered. "Sort of. She's the one who suggested I look into hiring someone, and then Tom at the elevator suggested Ada. She was the head cook at the schools here for a long time."

"She definitely knows how to keep a bunch of hungry cowboys happy."

"That she does," Jake agreed. The dinner bell he'd had installed on the porch rang. "Make sure the others heard it and go on in. I'll be there in a few minutes."

Gary nodded and walked away, while Jake scanned the horizon. Beginning to worry about Erin and Jonah, he smiled with relief when he saw two riders approaching the corral from the west. "It's about time you two returned," he said when they dismounted and led the horses closer.

"We found a stray calf in that little ravine up north," Erin explained. "It took us a while to get him out. He's with his mama now, and I hope she keeps a better watch on him." She turned to Jonah and held out her hand. "I'll take the horses to the barn and make sure they're cooled down."

"That's okay," Jonah answered.

It hadn't escaped Jake that Erin hadn't yet looked directly at him. "Come on, Jonah," he said, "let's get some of that dinner Ada fixed. Erin won't be long, I'm sure."

"Only as long as it takes," she said, taking the reins from Jonah.

Jake watched her lead the horses away, then crooked a finger at Jonah. "Let's go."

"Something's bothering her. Maybe if you—"

"She gets moody sometimes," Jake said, remembering a much younger Erin. "She'll be fine. When she's ready to talk, she will."

With a shrug of his shoulders, Jonah followed Jake into the house and took a seat at the table with the others. But Jake felt restless, unsettled, as he joined them.

"You two are a little late," Ada said, placing a bowl of fluffy mashed potatoes on the table. "And where's Miz Erin?"

"Putting the horses away," Jake answered.

Ada slowly shook her head. "Maybe you'd better go give her a hand, Mr. Jake."

"You're probably right," he said, pushing away from the table. "A little help will make it go faster. Be sure there's something left for us."

When Ada promised she would, Jake went to the barn. He found Erin in a stall near the end, grabbed a brush and started to help.

"You don't need to do that," she said.

"I know," he answered, "but Ada thinks you need to eat."

"I'm not really hungry."

He stopped brushing. "You? Not hungry? Damn, Erin, you've always been able to put away as much as the rest of us. No one would know it, though, looking at you." He ran an admiring eye over her slim but curvy figure.

As if she knew he watched her, she turned

to look at him. "I'm glad you're here, Jake. I needed to tell you something, and now is as good a time as any."

"I knew something was bothering you."

"Nothing's bothering me, but..." Her chest rose and fell with a deep breath. "This is my last day here, Jake."

He pulled his gaze up to hers. "I don't think I heard you right. I thought you said—"

"I did."

He didn't know whether to be surprised or angry, but the latter began to win. "You're quitting?"

She nodded. "It's time."

"Time to quit? Why? You're not a quitter, Erin. You never have been." But she had. She'd quit racing. Or had she? "What are you going to do?"

"There's a rodeo in Chandler this weekend," she said. "I'm meeting up with some friends, and—"

"Why go back? Even you said it's a hard life."

She finished the grooming and put the brush away. "Because I have to."

Anger bubbled deep inside him. "That doesn't make sense."

"It would, if you were me." She leaned against the side of the half wall. "I need to prove myself again, as much for me as for anyone else. I'm not a quitter, Jake. You should know that."

He did. He'd even said it. He'd seen her determination when they were kids, watched her spend hours training and practicing. And she'd been good. He knew that, too. "But you've already proven yourself."

She shook her head. "One more time. That's all I need. I know I can do it. Maybe not Nationals, but MacDuff is ready. And so am I. If I don't do it now—"

"I've never known such a bullheaded woman," he said, unable to look at her.

"Determined, Jake," she corrected. "I'm determined to go out on a high note."

He hadn't stopped her before. He wouldn't

stop her this time. If she wanted to go back to the circuit, he had to let her, the same way he did before. He wouldn't crush her dream. He knew how that felt. He had his now, most of it, anyway, and she wanted to go back to hers. How could he stop her?

But he wanted to. He wanted so bad to stop her. And then that old feeling he'd had the night he told her he wouldn't be back, that they were over, came back again, along with the anger that had gotten him through it.

He slammed out of the stall, causing the horse to shy, but he turned back. "Okay. Go. That's what you want, that's what you get. Stop by and say howdy sometime when you're in the area."

"I will," she answered.

He took three steps toward the big barn door and saw Jonah standing there. "What do you want?" he growled.

"I want you two to stop being so selfish and pigheaded," Jonah answered, walking toward him. "I don't think I've ever known anybody as stubborn as you two are, except maybe my dad. Stop blaming each other. I came here because I wanted to meet the people who gave me life. I wanted to meet the girl who wrote a letter thanking the two people who would raise me and be the parents the two of you couldn't be."

Jake shook his head. "This would have happened whether you'd come or not. Erin wants to rodeo. That's the end of it."

"And you call her stubborn," Jonah said.

Jake heard the sound of boot heels on wood behind him but ignored it. "You don't know what you're talking about."

"You don't think so?" Jonah asked. "Okay, then. But if the two of you can't admit that you love each other and make it work out between you two, I'm out of here."

Jake sighed. "It won't work, Jonah." He turned to look at Erin, who stood there, white-faced. "I'll cut you a check before the end of the day."

Her chin came up. "Give it to my brothers." Without another word, she brushed past him and walked out, while he and Jonah stared after her.

Jonah turned back to him. “Wow. You sure don’t know much about women.”

Jake couldn’t argue. When it came to Erin, he didn’t know anything.

Chapter Eleven

"What are you doin', girl?"

Erin looked up from stowing things away for the drive and saw Ada in the doorway of her motor home. "I'm competing in a rodeo tomorrow in Chandler," she announced, smiling.

"What for?"

Erin had begun to wonder the same thing. "To win, hopefully," she answered, doing her best to maintain the smile.

Ada lowered herself onto the easy chair. "So I heard."

Chuckling softly, Erin put her extra boots in the closet where she could grab them quickly if needed. "Then why did you ask?"

"Because I didn't believe it."

"Now you know it's true."

"Erin Walker, you look at me."

Wishing she didn't have to, Erin did as Ada said.

"Stop trying to smile like you're happy," Ada grumbled, "because I know you aren't. I'm not a fool like some people. I know the people I care about."

"I know," Erin whispered. But some people—one in particular—didn't know her as well as they thought they did. "It's what I'd planned, Ada, before I even pulled in the lane last February."

"Plans can change if the right thing comes along."

Erin gave her a sideways glance. "You mean the right person, don't you?"

Ada waved away the question with her hand. "Thing, person, it doesn't matter. What matters is in your heart."

"So I heard."

"Don't you throw my words back at me, girl," Ada warned. "I know what I'm talking about. The mister and I had our own hard times, but when it came right down to it, love made the difference."

Unable to clear the lump in her throat, Erin nodded.

"Now, Jake is actin' like a bull in a china shop, stompin' around the house, and only the good Lord knows what's goin' on inside him. But outside? I saw the men scattering when he headed their way."

"He's a little upset," Erin managed.

"Upset? That man is *angry*."

Erin nodded. "At me."

"Maybe, but I'm not so sure."

"I am."

"Then there's that boy of yours, Jonah. He's wearin' a scowl almost as mean as Jake's." When Erin didn't reply, she went on. "You're gonna lose the two best things in your life, honey, if you don't do somethin'."

Frustrated, Erin dropped to the sofa. "It's not my place to do anything. I've done all I can. The ball, as they say, is in Jake's court."

Silence dragged on for what seemed like an eternity, and then Ada spoke. "He loves you, honey."

Erin pushed down the hope that sprang to life. "Did he tell you that?"

"He didn't have to tell me," Ada said. "I see it in his eyes every time he looks at you. And I see the same in yours."

Erin didn't argue. She did love him, but maybe too much. And maybe she had too much pride. She couldn't explain it to Ada, though. Or Jake. If she could, maybe they could fix this.

"Go see him before you leave," Ada said, shoving slowly to her feet. "Tell him what's in your heart."

Shaking her head, Erin stood. "Jake and I have already said all there is to say. I'm going, he's staying. That's where it ends."

"You're chasin' the wrong dream," Ada said

from the doorway. "You already did that, and you're too stubborn to let it go."

"I want to go back to the circuit and prove myself," Erin said, a little louder than she meant to. "I want to be a winner. Don't you understand?"

"Honey, you've always been a winner," Ada said softly, "to everyone who's ever known you. You don't have to prove anything. Not to me, and surely not to folks who don't know you, except as some little thing that rides a horse around some big ol' barrels. Search your heart for what it is you really want, then go after it. Do whatever it takes to get it, just like you did with your racin'."

But Erin didn't feel she did get it with her racing. In another year or two, she would be one more unknown. Younger girls had been stepping up, long before she gave up and came home. Even Shelly had mentioned it more than a year ago and again recently.

"That's what I'm doing," she told Ada. "I'm doing whatever it takes to get what I want."

With her hand braced on the door frame, Ada studied her. "Are you sure you want to live that hard life again? Is that what you really want?"

Erin tried to answer but couldn't, so she nodded.

Ada's loud sigh seemed to bounce off the walls. "Then come give me a hug. I don't know when I might be seein' you again, so it'll have to last a long while."

Smiling, Erin walked to the door and slipped her arms around Ada's ample waist as Ada enveloped her in a motherly hug. "I'll miss you, Ada," Erin said, trying not to cry. "And I'm sorry I can't do what you want me to do."

"It's not what I want you to do, child, it's what you want to do. It's whatever is in your heart."

Stepping out of the embrace, Erin nodded. "Thank you, Ada. Nobody knows how to talk to me the way you do. You've always been there when I've needed you the most. And this time

I'll stop by to see you when I'm in the area. I promise."

Pressing her palm to Erin's cheek, Ada smiled. "I know you will."

"Let me see if Dylan will loan me his truck, and I'll drive you back."

Ada waved her away. "I drove my old car over here. It's sittin' there by the big house, and your brother was nice enough to show me where you're livin'. I'll go back the same way I came."

Erin stood in the doorway and watched until Ada disappeared around the far side of the house. She'd barely had a chance to spend time with her good friend, but she would make some time whenever she could.

With a sigh, she returned to packing things away so they wouldn't fly around her on a bumpy road. But the sound of her phone ringing made her stop. Picking it up, she saw Shelly's number displayed and answered with a smile.

"What are you doing?" Shelly asked.

"Battening down the hatches," Erin said,

laughing, and hoping Shelly wouldn't notice that she wasn't as happy as she should be.

"Good. I was afraid you might have changed your mind."

"No, I'll meet you at the campground early in the morning. I probably won't sleep a wink tonight."

"I'm glad you're excited. We've reserved a space for you next to our RV, so you don't have to worry about finding one."

Erin pushed everything from her mind except the hour drive and the rodeo itself. "That will make it easier."

"Is everything all right?" Shelly asked.

"Everything is fine," Erin answered.

"Okay, but if something happens or you change your mind—"

"I won't."

"Then we'll see you tomorrow," Shelly said, and ended the call.

Still trying to forget everything that no longer mattered, Erin went back to work. By tomorrow at the same time, she would be in the saddle, making sure MacDuff was ready. Together, they would be winners.

JAKE WATCHED ADA park her car, then walk up the porch steps and into the kitchen. "Did you forget something?" he asked her.

"No," she said, grabbing her starched apron and tying it around her. "I went to tell a friend goodbye."

"You tried to talk her out of going, that's what you did."

"No, sir, I did not. Erin does what she wants, and nobody can make her do otherwise."

He had no argument for that. "Good."

"I only told her to search her heart for what she really wanted," Ada continued. "And I'll tell you now to do the same thing. That's all I have to say about it. Now why don't you sit down and eat somethin'. All that growlin' and stompin' makes a person hungry."

"Not me," he replied. "I'm just fine."

He turned to leave the kitchen, but as he did, he heard her mutter, "I can see just how fine you are, and it isn't good."

Nobody seemed to understand that going after Erin would be the worst thing to do. He loved her. He always had. Tying her down when she wanted to be free would be bad for both of them. He wouldn't stop her, no matter what Ada or Jonah or even Gary and the crew had to say. Erin would do what she wanted to do. Only then would she be happy. Experience and mistakes had taught him that.

In his small office, he settled at his desk, planning to catch up on the book work he'd left undone for too long. But the sound of a vehicle interrupted his plan, and he looked out the window to see Dylan's truck. "Not now," he said, wishing for the solitude he craved.

Stepping out onto the porch from the side door, he waved as both Dylan and Luke climbed out of the truck. When they walked around the porch, after saying hello to Ada, he met them and invited them into his office. "I should have known you'd show up. Everybody thinks they can fix things."

Dylan frowned at him. "The only one who can fix this is you."

"I tried. It didn't work."

"Then try again," Luke said. "Erin has her pride, but—"

"And so do I." Jake wished he hadn't said that. His pride wasn't what kept him from going to Erin and begging her not to leave. "She's been planning to go back since she got here. Did you know that?"

Shaking his head, Dylan answered, "No, but I'm not surprised. But I thought—"

"We both thought she'd change her mind," Luke finished. "Especially because of you and Jonah."

"Well, she didn't," Jake stated. "And she won't."

Dylan's frown deepened. "Don't be so sure.

She may be stubborn, but when it comes to people she cares about—"

"Did you try to talk to her?" Jake asked.

"We did."

"And?"

Dylan shrugged.

"She's made up her mind," Luke said, and leaned against the desk. "And you're the only one who can change it."

"No," Jake replied. "I can't. I won't even try. So you two might as well go back home, treat your ladies to something special tonight and tell your sister goodbye with a smile."

"Women," Dylan said with a grunt. "Can't live with 'em and can't stay sane without 'em. How'd they get such a hold on us? Makes me crazy sometimes."

"You have to know how to handle them," Luke said.

"Is that right?" Dylan asked him. "And you're an expert on this, I guess."

"No. No expert. But there has to be something." He looked from one to the other. "Maybe we could go to Chandler and watch her ride. If she knows she has our support, she might give in."

"Or not," Jake said, "unless you want to follow her around to every rodeo thinking she might finally give it up and come home. I'm telling you guys, she'll only dig her heels in deeper."

"I have a better idea," Dylan said.

Jake didn't know if he really wanted to hear it, but went along with it anyway. "What's that?"

"Lou's." When neither Jake nor Luke responded, Dylan explained. "We go now and stay until it closes."

"And that will do what?" Jake asked.

"Get you through this day, and tonight you'll either be too drunk to care or passed out until Erin is well on the road to Chandler."

"What time is she leaving in the morning?" Jake asked.

"About seven," Dylan answered. "It's an hour

drive, maybe more pulling a horse trailer with an RV, but she probably wants to check out the arena early and get in a little practice."

Or something else, Jake thought. "She's meeting a friend."

"She has a lot of them on the circuit, some of them barrel racers like her," Luke pointed out. "So what do you think? Send your wranglers home early and go to Lou's?"

"What about Glory and Hayley?"

"If we explain, they'll understand. Right, Dylan?"

Dylan stared at him. "We have to explain?"

"No," Jake said, "you don't. In fact…" He moved around to behind his desk and pulled open a drawer, then set a bottle of fine bourbon on the desk. "There's beer in the kitchen and anything else you'd like in the liquor cabinet."

Luke looked at Dylan. "Sounds like a plan."

Dylan agreed with a nod.

Jake pulled three tumblers out of the desk and

placed them next to the bottle. "I'd say we have everything we need except a little ice."

"In the kitchen?" Luke asked, pushing away from the desk and heading for the door. "I'll get some beers, too, if anyone wants any."

Dylan and Jake shook their heads.

"Suit yourselves," he said with a shrug, and walked out.

"How about a little music?" Jake asked, and reached behind him to turn on his system. "Any requests?"

"Garth, George, or something newer. Anything that isn't that weepy stuff."

"You got it." With the punch of a button, the room filled with the sound of fiddles, guitars and country twang.

They both looked up when Luke hurried into the room, balancing a six-pack of beer in one hand and an ice bucket in the other. "Look out. We've been nailed."

Ada appeared in the doorway, her hands on

her hips and a scowl on her face. “What are you boys up to?”

“Havin’ a little party,” Dylan answered.

“Oughta be a wake,” she muttered. “If you’re gonna be drinkin’, let me get you some food. Then I’m goin’ on home to watch me some television.” Turning around, she closed the door behind her and was gone.

“She doesn’t seem to appreciate a celebration,” Dylan said, causing the other two to laugh.

“I heard that,” came from the other side of the door.

“Hey, Ada,” Jake called out, “would you let t he men know to stop by my office before they leave?” When he didn’t get an answer, he shrugged.

“Do you want to send them home?” Luke asked, popping the tab on a beer can.

“Gary will be by soon if he doesn’t see me outside. We can always invite him and the others to join us.”

Dylan looked around the room as he filled two glasses with ice and liquor. "I don't think there's room in here."

"You're right," Jake agreed. "Let's keep it to family."

Dylan handed Jake a glass and lifted his own. "To family."

The others followed suit, then tipped up their drinks. "Now that's what I call smooth," Dylan said. "But I can't have much. And don't mention it to Glory or Erin. I'd never hear the end of it."

"Why's that?" Jake asked, shoving his desk chair into the middle of the room.

"I did a bit of drinking before Glory set me straight. I hate to say it, but she was right."

"They always are," Luke said. "Trouble, too. But it's hard to live without them, and I wouldn't trade Hayley for all the money in the world." He took another drink of his beer. "Hey, remember that time…"

Three hours later, after the wranglers had been sent home and the three of them had dredged up old memories, good and bad, Jake stared at his half-filled glass. It was only his second one—and he found he enjoyed the company more than the liquor. But it was enough to make him think in circles—until he remembered what else he'd stashed in his desk drawer.

He stood and rounded his desk, then pulled out another drawer and took out the high-heeled shoes Erin had left in the barn. "I'll be right back," he said, and started for the door.

"Going somewhere?" Luke asked.

"For a walk," he answered. "But stay and enjoy the refreshments. I won't be gone long."

"I'll bet he's going to see Erin," he heard Luke say, but he didn't hear Dylan's response.

Outside, the heat hit him, and he looked up at the sky, the sun edging closer to the horizon. Night would be along soon enough, and he thought about going back inside to finish off that half glass and more.

Instead, he started walking and soon found himself close enough to Erin's RV that he could see her loading things into the horse trailer sitting next to it.

He needed to wish her good luck, if nothing else. He didn't want bad feelings between them. But would it make it worse? Either way, he had to do it.

ERIN HEARD THE crunch of twigs and the snap of a small limb behind her as she shoved another bale of hay into the trailer. She didn't look to see what had caused the noises, suspecting Sollie had come to visit and tell her goodbye. Not that the dog had a clue she was leaving, but thinking so made her feel better.

"So, you're going."

She nearly jumped out of her skin and spun around. Jake stood at the edge of the tree line, his hands in his pockets, his face showing no emotion.

"I thought we already said goodbye," she replied.

"If you want to call it that."

She bent down to pick up two covered grain buckets. "I'll be back again, Jake."

"And we can pick up where we're leaving off?" he asked.

She didn't look at him but lifted the buckets and put them in the trailer. "If that's what you want."

"What I want is for you to stay," he said, his voice sounding closer. "But I can't stop you from leaving, Erin. I won't do that."

She straightened and faced him. He knew how to push her buttons, and she tried to control her temper. He could have stayed home and saved them both from this, but he didn't.

"Why not?" she asked. When he shook his head, she silently counted to five. "One of us has to know."

"Everything I've ever done, I did with good intentions," he said. "Breaking it off with you was one of those."

Her legs seemed unable to hold her. Lowering herself to the end of the trailer, she pulled in a shaky breath. "Why is that?"

He moved to sit beside her, clasping his hands to dangle between his knees. "I was fifteen when I realized I'd fallen for you. But it had happened long before that. Maybe that day you smacked the rump of my horse, and it took off while I hung on for my life. Do you remember that?"

Nodding, she relaxed and smiled. "Your uncle finally said you could take one of his horses out. But not before Dylan and I convinced him that you could ride. Which you couldn't. I'd never met anyone so determined in all my life. Except me, of course."

"That's what I liked about you. After that first summer I spent here, I didn't want to go home. Knowing I had summers here became the only thing that got me through the school year."

"I'm surprised," she said, "considering how mean I was to you."

"I didn't care. You didn't ignore me."

"I couldn't," she said with a shrug. She'd been as drawn to him as he had been to her. "And I didn't know why, until I was twelve and realized I wanted you to like me."

He lowered his head. "I wish I'd known that."

She felt the old embarrassment she'd had back then. "I couldn't let you know. I didn't know how."

They sat in silence for several minutes before he spoke again. "I guess I owe you an explanation."

When he took her hand and held it, she looked up. "For what?"

"For what I did…what I said that last night."

Not knowing if this would be good or bad, she couldn't respond. She didn't want to hurt anymore. Better to be done with it and move on. That's what she'd always done, and it had served her well. It would again.

His body rose and fell with a deep breath. "I never planned to go to college. But my parents had other ideas. I fought them about it.

Threatened to leave. I wanted to come back here and stay with Uncle Carl. Learn how to be a rancher, not a businessman like my dad. In the end, Uncle Carl took my choice away after my mother talked to him. And they won."

She stared at his hands, hands that knew every inch of her and more. It was her turn to explain why she'd done what she did.

"That last summer, you said you'd be back as often as possible, so when you came back at Thanksgiving, I thought everything was okay. I wanted you to know how much I—" She wouldn't say it. Couldn't. "I worried that you'd find somebody better than me in college. Somebody pretty, who didn't argue with you all the time or spend her life on a horse. I didn't know how to tell you, so I seduced you. I know it was a crazy, stupid thing to do, but I didn't care. And then when you—"

He turned his head to look at her. "I never meant a word of it, Erin. But I had to do it. Not just because my parents forced me to go to college. You deserved more than a visit from me every few months."

Gazing into his gray eyes, she saw regret and a sadness she'd never seen there before. "I wouldn't have minded."

"I needed more than that, Erin. Much more. I broke it off with you because I had to. For you."

He took her hand in his, and she felt his thumb move across her knuckles, sending warmth through her. She tried to ignore it but failed. "I don't understand."

"I wasn't nice about it. I didn't know how to do it any other way. You would have argued with me."

She turned away, knowing it was true. She would have done anything to keep him there. "But that doesn't explain it. We could have had spring break and summers, and—"

"Look at me, Erin, because I'm going to tell you why I did and said what I did. Why I was so angry that night." When she refused, he put a finger under her chin and forced her to look at him. "I wanted you to have the chance to do what you always wanted to do—join the rodeo and travel." He shook his head. "I didn't tell you that, and maybe I should have. When it came to what I wanted, my parents didn't give me a choice about college. They put a lot of pressure on me, keeping me from what I truly loved—being with you. I wanted to give you what I hadn't been given. I wanted you to have the freedom to chase your dream."

Erin's throat clogged with tears, and she ducked her head so he wouldn't see. "We were too young," she managed to say.

"You were, but I wasn't. I was eighteen. I could have walked away from my parents and what they wanted. I didn't. Not for two years, anyway. And by then, I didn't care. I'd lost what I wanted. I wanted *you*. But it was too late. So I left school. I knew Uncle Carl wouldn't budge on letting me come here, so I went out to Arizona and found a job on a ranch. That's why

I hired Jonah when you didn't want me to. I wanted to give him a chance."

"I should have guessed," she whispered, her heart breaking for what he'd been through.

"I was never happier than when I was here," he said. "That's why I came back. I could have sold the ranch, bought a new one somewhere else, but this is where I wanted to be. Even knowing you wouldn't be here."

"But I am," she said.

"And you're leaving."

Not knowing what to say, she remained silent and noticed that dusk had darkened the sky. She would be on the road in a few hours, headed to Chandler. Back to rodeo.

He took her hand again. "Look at me, Erin."

She did, but it didn't calm her or make any of it easy.

"I've always loved you, Erin," he said, his gaze holding hers. "I never stopped loving you."

She opened her mouth to tell him she loved him, too, but nothing came out. Speechless at the declaration, she closed her eyes. When she opened them and saw the love in his, hers stung with tears. "Oh, Jake." She sighed.

He kissed her, a kiss she would never forget. One filled with sweetness and love.

"Hold on a minute," he said when they took a breath. He stood and started walking toward the trees.

"Are you leaving?" she asked, feeling a prick of panic.

"No," he said, and looked over his shoulder at her. "I'm never leaving."

He disappeared out of sight, and she heard rustling. She waited, wondering what he might be doing. When she finally saw him heading back to her, she saw what he was carrying. "My shoes!" she said, snatching the high heels he dangled in front of her. "Where did you find them?"

"I didn't. Kelly did. In the barn." When she groaned, he laughed. "Don't worry. I told him some story about teenagers necking in the barn, and he believed it. But you might want to think up some story, if he ever sees you in them."

She laughed, and then noticed a small box stuffed in one of the shoes. "What's this?"

"Open it," he said, watching her.

Curious, she did. Nestled inside was a sparkling diamond ring. She looked up to see him smiling, yet tentative.

"Will you?" he asked. "Will you marry me, Erin?"

Unable to speak, she nodded, tears of happiness stinging her eyes, and then she threw her arms around him. Years of loneliness on the road, without Jake in her life, flashed through her mind. *Those days are gone.*

"When?" he whispered in her ear. "Soon?"

"Very soon," she whispered back.

Taking her hand, he slipped the ring on her finger. "I considered a branding iron," he said, "but I guess this will have to do."

"I'm relieved," she said, laughing. Smiling,

she looked into his eyes. "It's beautiful, and you're wonderful."

He stood and helped her from the trailer, and they shared another kiss, full of love and unspoken promises.

"You can rodeo all you want," he told her, "but you have to come home, not wander the country. At least, not without me. So come home when you've won in Chandler."

She'd nearly forgotten. "Hold that thought," she said, pulling her phone from her pocket. She hit a button and waited.

"Shelly," she said, when her friend answered, "I'm sorry to call you so late, but I won't be in Chandler tomorrow."

Jake grabbed her and swung her around, as Shelly said, "Oh, I'm sorry to hear that. Did something happen?"

"Yes," Erin answered, stifling a giggle, while trying to hush Jake's whoops and hollers. "I'm engaged."

Shelly screamed so loudly that Erin had to

hold the phone away from her ear. Jake laughed, but she shushed him. "I'll send you the money you spent for the entry fee."

"No, you won't," Shelly said. "Consider it an engagement gift. Money well spent, I'd say."

Erin laughed. "All right. And I'll call you tomorrow."

"Tell her we'll try to be there on Saturday," Jake whispered.

"I heard that," Shelly said. "We look forward to meeting a guy who has to be special. After all, he picked you. Now go on, enjoy."

Erin slipped the phone back into her pocket and looked at Jake. "How long have you had this?" she asked, wiggling her finger with the ring on it.

"A few days," he answered with a devilish smile. "*Before* you told me you were leaving."

"I'll bet Jonah will be surprised in the morning."

Jake snorted. "Somehow I doubt it. He's a pretty smart kid."

"A pretty smart young man," Erin corrected. "Maybe it's because he takes after you."

"Could be," Jake agreed with a laugh. Running a finger down her cheek, he sighed. "I wonder what he'd think of a baby sister."

"I think he'd like that. He's an only child."

"Not for long," Jake said softly.

She had a sudden thought and groaned.

"What?" he asked.

"I have to plan a wedding!"

"Heaven help us," he said, laughing again.

"I love you, Jake Canfield."

He grinned, and then kissed her. "That's good, Erin Walker, because I love you, too."

Epilogue

Jonah couldn't remember being as happy as he'd been when he realized he'd found Jake and Erin. A second set of parents. Looking back, finding them had been easy. Not that it had seemed like it, but he'd been lucky. And it all started with a letter.

He'd climbed into the attic, looking for his old Cub Scout handbook. He'd forgotten some of the knots he'd been taught and knew the instructions were in the book. He had to hunt around the attic, but he found it in a box with his name printed on it. His mom was good about doing that. Along with the book were a few baby clothes, old school papers and photos of him. And the letter.

Curious, he'd pulled it out. It had been written in a bold, wide scrawl that began with the words, "I don't know who you are, but I want to tell you thank you for adopting my baby son." He'd continued reading and came away knowing she had loved him and wanted only the best for him. That's when he knew he had to find her. But first, he'd battled with his parents. When they wouldn't give him the answers he wanted and his dad yelled at him, he started searching with the help of a friend. And now—

"We are gathered here together..."

The sound of Reverend Baker's voice brought him out of his thoughts as he stood under the flowered arch near the pond with the rest of the wedding party. He tried to pay attention, but it wasn't easy. He thought of all the things he'd learned, working for Jake, and how pretty Erin had looked, walking down the aisle toward them. He'd expected Jake to be nervous. Weren't grooms supposed to be on their wedding day? Not Jake. He looked cool, calm and happy.

From his spot next to Jake, he could see his parents sitting in the second row, smiling and whispering. His mother had been excited about being invited to the wedding. His father had been pleased that his escapade in Oklahoma had turned out so well. Jake was the opposite of his dad, who decided he liked Jake after all, especially when Jake gave him a tour of the ranch. His dad loosened up a little. Everything had worked out great, and he always felt proud when introducing both sets of his parents. He couldn't have been happier.

"Jonah?"

Looking up, he saw Jake grinning at him. "Yeah?"

"The ring?"

He suddenly realized where he was and fished

for Erin's wedding ring in his tuxedo pocket, then handed it to Jake.

With the ring in hand, Jake leaned over to Jonah. "I'm glad you're here," he whispered.

"Me, too," Jonah whispered back.

Turning his attention to the minister, Jonah listened to words he'd heard a few times before about the symbol of the endless circle, and then Erin and Jake slipped the rings on each other's finger, saying the words, "With this ring…" He kind of liked that.

When the time came for Erin and Jake to kiss, he didn't feel embarrassed. This was what he'd wanted since the first moment he'd realized who these two people were and that they loved each other. He took a quick look at his mom and dad, who were holding hands. His mom, still smiling, wiped her eyes with a tissue, and his dad gave him a thumbs-up. Jonah couldn't remember his dad ever smiling so big.

He had a feeling his own smile might be even bigger.

The reception, along with a dinner and dance, followed at the Big Barn by the Commune, and he finally had a chance to tell Erin how happy he was for her and Jake. Himself, too.

"It might not have happened if it weren't for you," Erin said as they danced together. "Thank you for making me fess up to Jake."

Embarrassed, he ducked his head for a second. He'd only done what he thought was right. "You would have anyway."

Erin laughed. "Maybe. But I'm so proud of you, Jonah. Jake and I both are. And I'm so glad we've been able to meet your parents. I like them. I really do."

He shrugged the shoulder where her hand rested. "Yeah, they're pretty good parents. Even better now that they know you and Jake. I guess I'm one of the lucky ones."

"We all are." She looked at Jake standing with Bowie McClure, the friend who had bought some of Jake's land and started building on it. Then she focused on Jonah again. "If I haven't said it yet, you're something else."

Before he could answer, he felt a tap on his shoulder and turned to see who it was.

"My turn," Jake said, pretending to scowl at him. Jonah knew he didn't mean that mad look, because of the crinkles around his eyes.

"Not yet," Erin told Jake. "You'll have plenty of time later."

"A lifetime won't be enough."

Right then, watching the two of them looking at each other, he understood what love meant. "Are you two ever going to stop arguing?"

Jake laughed and Erin shook her head. "If we did, we'd know we were in trouble," she said.

Nodding, he released her and stepped away, while Jake put his arms around her. "Okay, but don't leave without saying goodbye," he told them.

They promised they wouldn't, and while he watched the two of them dancing, he had a feeling that there would be a lot of laughing and arguing in their life together, with lots and lots of love. He hoped that someday he would be just as lucky.

* * * * *